Conflict

Conflict

C Owen King

Best Wishes
Owen King

ATHENA PRESS
LONDON

CONFLICT
Copyright © C Owen King 2008

All Rights Reserved

No part of this book may be reproduced in any form
by photocopying or by any electronic or mechanical means,
including information storage or retrieval systems,
without permission in writing from both the copyright
owner and the publisher of this book.

ISBN 10-digit: 1 84748 068 3
ISBN 13-digit: 978 1 84748 068 2

First published 2008 by
ATHENA PRESS
Queen's House, 2 Holly Road
Twickenham TW1 4EG
United Kingdom

Printed for Athena Press

The boy led the way up the stony path to the rough stone steps, over which light spilled out of an open doorway. The light flickered from an old kerosene lamp on to a group around the doorway. The people spoke in hushed voices and cleared a way for Mrs Weston and the boy. As they climbed the steps in to the front room they could hear the stertorous breathing coming from behind the partition separating the living room from the bedroom. Lucille was in the front room speaking to two other people. Mrs Weston glanced at her before going through to the bedroom. The boy stayed close behind her. On a low bed lay a thick-set frame with charred clothes and an open mouth, from which the sound of deep breathing came while the chest heaved in time with each breath. A candle stuck in a saucer gave all the light, and the contrast between white teeth and black burnt skin. Sarah Lawrence sat beside the bed on which her husband lay.

Mrs Weston placed a hand on her shoulder.

'Sarah, I have sent for the doctor. He'll be here soon.'

'Thank you, ma'am, but I have sent for the priest already.'

'Well, don't forget, if there is anything you want, send to the hotel for it. I'm glad to see Lucille is here to help you.'

Sarah nodded. Mrs Weston and the boy went out, and the small group crowding the doorway hushed for a moment and made way for them again.

Out through the trees the darkness stretched to a sky thickly clustered with stars, and down below in the valley the darkness was rent by the headlamps of cars and pricked by the lights from the windows of the houses. The boy liked these dark nights almost as much as the full-mooned unreality. He did not expect Mrs Weston to speak. He had told her how he had found Clifton

Lawrence, his grandfather. It did not seem possible it would have happened to such a man, whom he loved, feared and respected. He was in a cherry tree when Clifton came through the pasture. He was the only father the boy knew. Today was Good Friday. He had no right to be in the cherry tree so he kept very quiet. Lawrence was collecting branches and leaves in a pile. He set fire to this and climbed a neighbouring tree to trim off a few more branches. The tearing sounded off after the sharp firm strokes of the cutlass. Boy looked up and saw the sparks leap up as man and branch landed in the fire. He raced across the pasture.

Pa, he thought, *you should not work on Good Friday.*

Everyone knew that this was the worst day for working. He reached the fire, grabbed the legs and dragged the unconscious form from the flames, and raced to the house for help.

Pa ran the estate which was owned by Mrs Weston, who also owned the hotel at which the boy lived and worked. So next he went to Mrs Weston for help and told her his story. She phoned the doctor, Peter Weston, her son. He was out but she left the message, asking him to come as soon as possible, and set off with the boy.

Clifton Lawrence was a dependable man and one of the few people she could trust. Yet his family had caused her enough trouble. She glanced at Boy, her husband's son and Lucille's. She remembered the young girl coming to work at the hotel as a receptionist. She was intelligent and had a secondary education but that was the trouble with these people – primitive, childish, vicious. The scheming girl had got round Frank, looking for promotion, and got pregnant. Clifton Lawrence – she had not been sure how he would take it. Frank expected demands for money, but instead, Clifton refused any assistance. The girl was angry at the failure of her schemes and, after her child was born, went to work as a labourer on the roads to shame them all.

Her brother, Daniel, in America, had been most upset, and had written a nasty letter to Frank. That reminded her – she would have to send a cable to him.

Then Peter had returned and wanted to marry Lucille. God knows, she had enough troubles. She would have to pray for Clifton tonight and again at Mass tomorrow. She sighed and the boy looked up curiously. He was used to those long, brooding silences. Mrs Weston seldom spoke, except to give instructions, and she went to church everyday. He liked the cool quiet of that large stone building with the shadowed windows. He never went with her. He had his visions and his wonderful music but he was never certain whether he had dreamt it all. He was certain that he did not like Good Friday. He needed Christ to die for him but not to be humiliated, to fall and to be beaten. Tomorrow – glorious Saturday – the bells would ring and he would leap in to the water and be cleansed. Would Pa also be cleansed?

The lights of the hotel blazed at them as they turned the corner, and they walked up to the gate opening on to the drive. As they went in to the hotel, Mrs Weston stopped and spoke to the receptionist.

'Yes, Mrs Weston. Dr Weston phoned to say he was on his way and that he would call in at the hotel on his way back, and I sent the telegram to Dr Daniel Lawrence in Washington.'

Mrs Weston went in to the dining room to see that the guests were being served and to find out if there were any complaints. Frank was at a table with the red-haired American tourist, Janet Martin. She disapproved of this dining tête-à-tête with guests but Frank would not care about her disapproval. She wished Janet Martin would go home, but that pretty, vivacious girl seemed to stay for ever. She wondered why tourists always seemed to think it did not matter what they did abroad. This licence was a bad example, especially in a country where Europeans had striven for so long to set a good one. She went up to the table and told Frank about Lawrence.

'How bad is it?' he asked.

'It looks bad enough.'

'Well, I suppose we will have to pay for the wake. You had better arrange for food and drinks to be sent up.'

'Peter has gone to attend to him and I sent a cable to Daniel.'

'Why bother that boy? He has never cared for his father.'

'Yes, I suppose so. No one seems to care very much, but I saw Lucille there and the boy is feeling it. He burnt his hands.'

Concern showed for the first time on Frank's face. Joan Weston's face was bitter.

'I put some butter on to soothe them but Peter will see them when he comes in.'

'All right. Call me when he comes in.'

'Do you mind if I join you?' Mrs Weston rebelled.

Frank was surprised. 'I'm sorry. I did not realise that you had not eaten.' She sat down in silence.

It was Cupid who had been serving the Westons and Janet. One could always be sure of employment in hotels if one owned a name like Cupid, Friday, Utrice or Princess. Even Julie became July and Lilian, Lily. It all helped to create an atmosphere of primitive simplicity.

Cupid put the tray down and said to Julie, 'Fireworks for so! The old lady not taking it no more. She come in vex because Boy hurt, and find Frank making sweet eyes at Janet. You should hear she: "Mind if I join you…?", her voice cold, cold, cold. You never see the mister, so surprised, but he take it cool. "Certainly. I was not aware you had not eaten." '

'You lie man.'

'True, true, true. The old lady going to be boss now. Frank must be getting old.'

'It time he old. He have big grown-up children like Dr Peter and he still want to play with little women. Look what he do to Lucille, and the madam still look after the boy for him.'

'Lucille look for all she get, don't worry.'

'You have no shame for your own people. Why he can't stick to his own?'

'Eh, eh, all women the same to men, you know. What time you finish work tonight?'

'Not your business. I have me own man, thanks.'

'That taxi man! Well, he have car and I not able. It's walks for me or the dance at The Rainbow!'

Peter Weston looked at his patient and felt sorrow, pity and anti-climax. This was his father in a much broader sense than Frank Weston. He had been brought up on the estate with Daniel and Lucille as one of Clifton's family, and had felt admiration for the man circumstances had placed as the servant of a father he despised and hated. He had tried to help Lawrence so often before, and failed, and he was doomed to fail him again for the last time.

When he had gone away to study medicine he had enjoyed being abroad and had toyed with the idea of never returning. He had graduated and worked in various hospitals, performing surgery and planning to be a surgeon, but finally he had stopped studying because the call of the islands was too strong. He returned, promising himself he could always return to finish his studies.

When he had returned to practise medicine on the island, Lucille was a girl of twenty with a three-year-old son who was his half-brother. Lucille worked on the roads and seemed abandoned by everyone. He employed her as his receptionist and they became great friends. His parents were annoyed; his patients considered her his mistress and Clifton warned him. There were many conversations he remembered but this one he remembered most clearly:

'You are hurting yourself and helping no one.'

'What about Lucille and the boy? I like her and the boy needs a father. I want to marry her if she will have me.'

'Don't worry! She'll have you. She's a boss with no one to boss. She wants the white life with all the things arranged for her. Here, that is impossible, unless she marries you.'

'What about the boy?'

'Boy is coloured. He is well fed, he goes to school. He will grow up no worse for being illegitimate.'

'Why didn't you get out or do better?'

'It was different then. It's changing, but slowly. Boy is intelligent enough to make his disadvantages a spur, not brakes.'

'Keep an eye on him and I'll be grateful.'

He had not been readily convinced but gradually Lucille realised he was not making advances or responding to hers. Last year she had left and gone back to work as a labourer. She was again a martyr, a cast-off mistress.

The groan from the bed roused him. At least he need not suffer. Lucille walked in to the room.

'Is he waking up?'

'He might, but I would like him to sleep through the night. I am going to give him an injection.'

She looked angry.

'Are you happy now? First me, then my father, you and your family destroy.'

Sarah intervened, 'How is Boy?' They looked at her blankly.

'He hurt his hands pulling Clifton out of the fire.'

Lucille turned and hurried from the room. Peter picked up his bag, gave the injections and left instructions. 'I'll be back later. We have to put up an intravenous drip, change his clothes and clean him up. He is losing fluids rapidly. I think he may have had a stroke as well. We cannot tell until he recovers consciousness.'

Lucille walked down the road with the thought of injury to the boy troubling her. Yet she had not worried about him for years now, except as a weapon to hurt the Westons, and that would also hurt her father. She hated Pa for spoiling her plans, and more intensely since she had worshipped him before. As children, Daniel, Peter and herself had played so often around him and relied on his guidance. Then came the pregnancy. She had planned it so – to become a rich man's mistress was better than being a poor man's wife. Pa was dejected, called her a dishonest fool and pointed out that a woman's chances of holding power was by withholding favours. He was always so right and so sure of himself, but it never did any good.

She heard hurrying footsteps behind her and, turning, recognised Peter. That was the man who would have married her if her father had not interfered – a soft sentimental man who did not know whether he wanted to be a martyr or not. She waited for him.

'I hope Boy is not badly injured.'

'I did not know that you were interested.'

'When he was born, I swore I would never feed him. I was discharged from the hospital on a Sunday afternoon. I took him straight from there to the hotel. Then I placed him on a table with a note "Frank Weston's child." Pa did not understand that hate. Why is it that he would not hate? He had only pity for me and for Frank. You did not know that he pitied your father, his boss. Frank had told me that he would sack Pa if I caused trouble and would accuse him of theft if necessary, and I told Pa this in my anger. He replied, "Then he is as big a fool as you are, because his loss would be greater than mine." Peter, if Pa dies, I want Boy back.'

'You can come back as my receptionist if you want to.'

'No, thanks. I want nothing from your family. It is time Boy made friends of his own age. What was he doing in the fields by himself? Your family will not let him play in the village with the other boys. Already he is learning the lesson of black and white.'

'Why are you so bitter? I respected your father more than my own.'

'Yes. But even to you he is an exceptional man and you still accept the fact of one inferior and one superior race.'

'I don't, and neither did your father. But neither of us could do much about it except set an example. It is a slow way but conditions are improving.'

'Conditions are improving, but not because of people like you and my father. It is because of people like my uncle, who fight and force people to recognise their authority.'

'Lucille, there is no point in arguing. Here is the hotel. I will go in and look after Boy for you.'

'I want to come in and see him. I want to show him that I care about him.'

'We will let Dan know what has happened, and I am certain he will come down.'

Conflict

'What can he do when he comes down?'

'He can comfort your mother, and your father will be pleased to see him. Besides, he would want to be here.'

'There is no inheritance for him. Shouldn't a firstborn expect something? The house is your father's and the small piece of land at Grace will have to support my mother.'

'I don't think he expects an inheritance. As a doctor in the States he is well off enough.'

★

Boy's room was a small box room squeezed between the kitchen and the room in which the receptionist-cum-telephonist sat. It opened in to the kitchen and the receptionist's room so that he was readily available for messages, helping to carry baggage and for receiving the collected shoes in the morning to be cleaned. Peter Weston hated argument and steered Lucille to Boy's room. Boy was lying on the bed but he sat up as they came in.

'Why are you in bed so soon, John?' asked Peter.

'I wanted to sleep before my hands hurt much more, Uncle Peter.'

'Well, your mother was worried about you and she has come to see you. Let me see your hands.'

Lucille and Boy were always embarrassed when they met. Usually it was on the street and Lucille would ask about school, Pa and Ma. He called her Lucille but he usually managed to avoid using her name since he had discovered that she was his mother.

Now he held up his hands and all eyes solemnly inspected them. They were red and a few blisters had already formed. The burns were neither severe nor extensive. The act of pulling his grandfather out of the fire and turning him over had sufficed to put out most of the flames. Yet Peter required a ritual and sat down, opened his bag and took out cleaning material and bandages. He dressed the hands while Lucille scolded and lectured in turn.

Did it hurt much? He was foolish to stay by himself so much. What was he doing wandering around the estate by himself? Had he no friends? Did he think he was too good to play with the boys in town? How could he be happy if he kept trying to be different and did not seek company?

The boy looked meek but made no reply. Peter gave him an aspirin and left two others for him to take later.

At that moment Mrs Weston came in with Frank. The receptionist had called her when Dr Weston arrived, and she had summoned Frank. They were surprised to see Lucille but Mrs Weston quickly asked Peter about the boy.

Peter assured them that Boy had suffered no permanent damage but that it would be a fortnight before the burns would heal. Frank turned to Lucille.

'I'm sorry your father is badly hurt.'

'I'm sure you are. You are sorry to lose a good slave.'

'Lucille,' protested Mrs Weston.

'Yes, my father is a willing slave. He says that Europeans have the money, the land, the education and therefore are the bosses. He says one can only be equal if one has money, land and education. He is dying now in poverty to show how stupid and useless his life has been.'

Frank was shocked at her callousness.

'I have looked after your father all his life.'

'No. He has looked after you and your estate for the past thirty years.'

Peter touched Lucille's shoulder.

'Let us go now. You will have to help your mother tonight.'

They walked down the drive slowly, in silence. Peter reached his car and turned to Lucille.

'You are no slave.'

'No. I'm free to work, to change my master, and to emigrate like my brother.'

'Why don't you emigrate?'

'Perhaps I will. I have not before because I wanted to own my own land.'

'Like your uncle. I hope Daniel gives more to your father than the rest of the family.'

'Oh yes! Dan has been very useful. Apart from Christmas cards we never hear of him.'

Peter Weston watched her walk away, then he got in to his car.

He had to get back to the hotel but he would go home to eat before coming back.

He went to the hospital to collect gauze, intravenous fluids, cleansing material and drip sets. He returned to Clifton's house and cleaned and dressed the burns, and set up the intravenous fluids. Sarah Lawrence helped him clean her husband quietly and efficiently. He wondered what else he could do for her and asked her. She could not think of anything and he realised she was still in shock.

'You should have something to help you sleep tonight.'

'No, thanks. I need to look after him and speak to the people who are coming to try to see him.'

'He should not have any visitors apart from Lucille and yourself.' He tidied up, repacked his bag and left.

Boy lay on his bed and looked at his white-bandaged hands. How often had he wished to be Peter's brother. How often had he hated Lucille for being his mother. He could not remember, but at his age months seemed as long as years, and it seemed a long time. His childhood seemed happy enough. There were other children at school to play with – five hundred of them, eighty in his class – and he had moved rapidly through the whole school in three years. He was surrounded by the biggest and dullest of the pupils because his work was reliable and could be copied. He was expected to win the scholarship for the school this year. He had fewer problems at that school than the other children. He wore shoes, clean clothes, could own books, and this distinguished him from ninety percent of the school. The classes were separated from each other by about six feet of empty space. Long benches and desks were fronted by a blackboard, and in the back benches nothing could be heard but the roar of the school as one conglomerate noise of child-chatter and teacher-shouting. He had learnt to escape from school by slipping away at break-time, at first to watch cricket, and later for no reason, until one day Lucille saw him out during school hours. She had lectured him, just like tonight – except that she hurt him then.

'Niggers like you have only one chance – education – and you run away. It is no use preaching to people like you. You have to be taught a lesson.'

She had hauled him back to school, marched in, stopped the class and then harangued the teacher for allowing children to run away. Silence had settled on the whole school. The headmaster had come down from his desk on a raised platform at the end of the school. He promised to attend to the matter at once and Lucille retired. Boy was publicly flogged. He did not mention this humiliation to the Westons but he did not go swimming so often or playing in the back yards or the playing fields. He lived in dreams where he was important and loved, but he roamed around the hotel and the estate feeling betrayed and isolated. Only one person made him feel that love was possible and that was Pa, but Pa was not important or loved, so perhaps that did not count as much as the opinion of people like Mr Weston.

At one time he had wanted a dog. He remembered the time when he had wandered through the outskirts of town and noticed the sturdy dust brown dog walking in front of him. The animal was heavily pregnant and ambling along the pavement. It turned down a small alley then moved in under one of the houses. The house was a wooden shack that stood twenty inches above the ground on short, concrete pillars. The boy squatted and looked under the house and noticed the rough earth of the original terrain, one or two crab holes, a few pieces of wood, two or three bottles and an old shoe. The dog was scratching at the earth at one place where the under-house space narrowed down to about ten inches. The four-by-four beams also tended to diminish the available space. The dog lay down to test the comfort of the space.

Boy walked away thoughtfully. He wanted a dog, he needed a dog, but at the age of seven years no one was considering his wishes. He almost certainly would not be able to keep it at the hotel. The old dog at Pa's was not interested in playing or going on long walks. For the next week Boy watched that house. Twice he brought some meat bones or bread to throw under the house for the dog but he made no other attempt to become friendly with it. The following week he heard the tiny squeals of puppies but there was no movement that he could see.

The week after that, having made sure that the mother was away, he screwed up his courage to begin his crawl in to the depression. He did not want to reach out to areas which he had not yet inspected, for fear of centipedes or scorpions. So, using elbows and toes, he squirmed his way forward. It was only ten feet ahead. The further he went the more fearful he became, because the ground sloped upwards. He almost turned back but he could now see brown sausage bodies wriggling. Finally, he went forward, and could see the seven bodies tumbling over each other in the basin of earth. They were about six inches long and all shades of brown: red brown, khaki brown, brick brown, chocolate brown and golden brown. He watched a while and made no effort to touch them. It was time to go before he was caught.

He tried to turn around but the space was too low for that. He could not go forward because there was even less space there. For a moment he froze in panic. He then tried pushing on the beams above him, but finally he found the best way was to inch backwards, the way he had come. His head finally cleared the edge of the house, and he pushed himself to his knees.

'What you doing under my house?'

He looked around and there was a little old lady with white hair who looked small, wrinkled and ancient, but her voice was stern and her hands were on her hips.

'I am looking for my puppies.'

'You mean that brown dog yours?'

'No! But it has seven puppies and I want one of them.'

'What age they have?'

'About two weeks.'

'Well! In three to four weeks they will be walking about.'

'But they will be too small to take away.'

'Yes, but if you don't take yours somebody else will take it.'

'I will come back twice a week but I don't need to go back under the house again.'

So three weeks later he was there when the puppies were crawling around under the house, but they did not come out in to the open. The following day he met the old lady who told him that the puppies were walking about and would soon be following the mother. He made sure the big dog was not there and looked for the fluffiest he had chosen. He waited until it was close enough and grabbed. He thanked the old lady and took off home. Near the hotel he tucked it under his shirt and brought it in to his room. At first it was easy to feed it and clean up after it but after three weeks it was making too much noise to conceal it any more and he was ordered to remove it. He had no choice but to take it to Pa's. There followed many good weeks and months of walking his dog around the estate. It was well fed and exercised so it became a large strong dog. Even Pa said it was a good watch.

Peter Weston entered the hotel and saw his father sitting at a table in the corner of the lounge. He was smoking a cigar and opposite him was the pretty, red-haired American tourist. He walked up to the table and introduced himself to Janet Martin.

'How do you do, Miss Martin? Could you excuse my father for a moment? I would like a word with him.'

'All right, Peter. It's about Clifton and Lucille. Have a seat. Janet, Peter always feels obliged to be other people's guardian angel. Perhaps it is because he is a doctor, but I wonder why it is always the natives he has to keep under his wing.'

'Dad, I came to tell you Clifton is dying. I could not say it while Lucille and Boy were present.'

'So all your science and skill will be useless!'

'Yes, but with the right conditions and hospital facilities he might have a chance. Here he has none.'

'What is the matter with him?' asked Janet.

'He has severe burns,' replied Peter.

'And your hospital cannot treat him?'

'No, it is equipped to deal with minor conditions and nursing bed-ridden patients.'

'What happens to people needing more intensive treatment?'

'They go away if they can afford it, or they remain, and nature or the obeah man comes.'

'If I offered to pay for sending him to a hospital abroad, wouldn't it help?'

'No thanks. He requires emergency treatment,' said Peter.

'The obeah man is probably being consulted now,' said Frank. 'The order is: the doctor, the priest, the obeah man.'

'Is it necessary to sneer at a time like this? A man is dying. He has worked for you all his life, holidays and Sundays included, and has had very little in return in cash or respect. If an obeah man is being consulted it is because his bosses have failed him.'

'Bosses and rulers are always in a minority. They are always painted as harsh and cruel, yet they have a duty to their workers. They must produce to pay those workers and to produce they must have discipline. It is even worse with natives.'

'Stop calling them 'natives'. They are no more natives than you are. We are all imported here.'

'What's in a name, Peter? Let me call them Negroes. They are primitive, two or three generations removed from savages in Africa, most of them ignorant of their own fathers. They are like children – irresponsible – and I look after the ones who work for me. What else would you have me do? Call them equal? They are not. It has taken years for Western man to develop, industrialise and gain his superiority in education, management and technical matters. They are not ready for these things, but they are being given an opportunity to see these things for themselves. Ask Janet and she will tell you. She, being an American, probably has even more ideas on the subject. I want to go and see your mother. Have a drink while I am gone.'

Peter Weston gulped his drink down with a trembling hand and signalled the waiter for another. He looked at the appealing 'little-girl' face opposite him and asked, 'What are your ideas, or should we change the subject?'

'No, I would like to know about your work and your ideas, so I ought to give you mine. Unfortunately, I have not thought about it seriously. I know of the problem but it has never touched me. I have no objection to sharing a car, or a restaurant or a swimming pool with a Negro but I do not feel impelled to travel south of the Mason-Dixon Line and insist that he shares them with me. People here seem lucky to live in such a wonderful climate, so simple and so close to nature. Education might spoil this for them by making them think and act like people who live in a temperate climate. You know, making hay while the sun shines and storing nuts for the winter.'

'You are inconsistent, Miss Martin. The Negroes in America are already westernised and it is the Indians who live on reservations. It is important that people are educated. I mean, taught to read and given access to books and allowed to discuss these books in leisure time. Let them accept what they wish and reject the rest. But we have never attempted to provide reasonable schools and even the poorly equipped ones and poorly staffed ones we have are not too grossly overcrowded since attendance is limited. Children cannot be spared from the work at home or in the fields, cannot buy books, transport is poor and clothes are ragged. Yet despite this, now that we have libraries and television and jet aeroplanes, the world is shrinking and it will become apparent that western education is important and that mechanisation, industrialisation, and scientific studies are important steps in advancement of any nation. Manual labour will be replaced by mechanical labour.'

'Then why are you worried?'

'Because I wish to speed up this process and make use of all abilities in the community, so that the bitterness which exists at the moment can be erased before the world becomes zoned in to black and white or eastern and western.'

'Would that be bad?'

'Not at first, because we, the West, have bought out all the choice areas. Already we are surrendering all the untenable positions and moving out of them, but the time comes when we are left with areas we do not wish to move out of – South Africa, Southern Rhodesia – and we will have to find reasons for defending them.'

'Doctor, please call me Janet. Why do you let all this worry you? I am sure the new generation feel like you and that you will replace the old.'

'That is the counsel of Clifton, the man who is dying, but tonight I am not so certain. It sounds like surrender to drift.'

'That is simply depression. Now, drink up and take me out. I would like to see the nightspots.'

'Right then. Let us move out before Father returns to irritate us.'

Boy, still unable to sleep, could not avoid listening to this conversation. Usually the noise and bustle in the lounge made conversation blurred and indistinguishable. The adult world was still incomprehensible to him and he had long ago realised that he could not influence it. The obvious answer seemed to be the impossible to the adult. He had longed for Uncle Peter's marriage to his mother, for Uncle Dan to return from America, for his father to acknowledge him. He was not certain what was real and what was vision, what was ambition and what was dream. He had visions of his god and his queen and he walked in a world where he knew who bosses were only by their ability to order and to inflict punishment: the school teacher, the policeman, civil servant or estate owner. It did not appear to be a clear-cut distinction in black and white, of slave and master, but it did seem the higher the boss, the more widely acknowledged, the less need there appeared to be to demonstrate the power. He could appreciate a god made humble and that, in his case, humility could be a virtue and not necessity, that turning the other cheek demonstrated strength rather than weakness. Man's need to crucify himself or become drunk terrified him. The world was a testing time to qualify for heaven. He longed and prayed for the end of the test, or failing that, a transition to adulthood in order to withdraw from it all. Meanwhile he had his dreams and his visions. His queen was tall, slim, and regal; he had wondered whether her clothes were kept for museums. His classmate disillusioned him. His father was an immigrant so he knew. 'They burn them, man. You think anything that touched her can go to anyone else?'

Somehow that seemed wasteful, so he switched his vision to his Christ in flowing robes and crown of thorns. He too had been beaten to his knees today. His last escape was through his caves to Central Africa, to organise a backward tribe to train, to drill, to arm. He was not certain why he did this, except that it seemed good to have a secret army.

*

Peter Weston drove down the narrow, twisting road that wound in and out of the hills. The night was alive with the sounds of insects, and fireflies and moths splashed against the windscreen of the car. The girl lay back against the seat and looked at his serious face with amusement.

'Afraid of spoiling the image?'

'What do you mean?'

'Why this long drive in the country?' Is there something special at the end of it? Or do you want to avoid being seen in female company?'

'Well, it's Good Friday and there will not be much life anywhere tonight. This is a quiet nightclub and a good one.'

They drove up to the patio of a horseshoe bungalow, which was dimly lit. A few couples were dancing in the open space enclosed by the horseshoe. A slender youth in uniform invited them to sign the visitors' book. Peter promised to do so later and steered Janet to one of the many empty tables. A waiter took their orders and quickly reappeared with drinks.

'You surprise me, Peter. Do you come here often?'

'No. Life is too serious for this, except when it becomes too serious.'

'Will you please stop talking in riddles.'

'Let's dance then.'

They walked on to a tiled floor under the stars and danced. The soft slow music suggested a timeless eroticism which the surroundings did nothing to diminish. The faces of the passing couples were indistinct and the sound of chatter and laughter at the bar was subdued. The dance ended and they began to walk back to the table. A tall, thick-set man almost bumped in to them, excused himself, then recognised Peter.

'Hello, Doc, I didn't expect to see you here.'

'You surprise me even more, Mr Lawrence. I suppose you do know about your brother's condition?'

'I do know, but I cannot help him if you can't!'

'What about your constituents? Wouldn't they think it a bit odd?'

'Not if I had come to see the doctor and ask his opinion.'

'You had no idea I was here.'

'But Doc, any good reason is reason enough.'

'How different you and Clifton are.'

'Please introduce me and invite me to sit with you.'

'Certainly. Miss Martin, this is Mr Lawrence, the Minister for Health in the island's government.'

They sat at the table and Lawrence continued, 'Yes, my brother is a good conservative – a supporter of established order – an Uncle Remus. He is happy with the crumbs from the table.'

'I suppose you are ashamed of him.'

'Under conditions ten years ago he had an excuse, but even then it was a poor one. He has had no excuse since he and all the others like him had the vote. As a solid, respected citizen he has influence but he will not speak or vote for his kind. His employer rapes his daughter and he shrugs his shoulders. What I have achieved has been despite my brother. Would you have me weep now? No friend, I will wait for the funeral when an audience is present. Your father is a man I can deal with – he is the good old school and he will face great odds secure in the knowledge that if he cries out, help will come from abroad. You would have me forget all this and the years of insult and domination and say, "let's shake hands and be friends now that I am the majority." My brother would help you but your system has been killing him for a long time. Goodnight, Doc. Goodnight, Miss Martin.'

Janet sighed, 'I don't seem to be having much chance to say anything this evening. Just when you are about to become pleasant someone comes and makes speeches. Are you always so out spoken in your criticism?'

'No, but Lawrence always annoys me, especially when I compare him with his brother.'

'Is he a good Minister of Health?'

'That's not a very important necessity in an underdeveloped country. Public health is not medicine, it is simply making available the amenities of civilisation: water supply, good roads, electricity, good housing, good diet, education. By the time these are present you are no longer underdeveloped and you can afford to spend money on the sick and the dying.'

'Why are you so cynical? Don't your patients pay you?'

'They cannot afford to. You said they seem happy. They have no worries. They do not need mansions to live in or clothes to keep warm. The environment is on their side. Indeed, petty larceny is rife since food is the only basic need. Heavy punishment is imposed on offenders when caught. At one time it was necessary to cut down the fruit trees to make them work. They are paid pocket money like irresponsible children and all else is provided: medicine, school, church, love. They do not expect to have to pay for these since they cannot afford to. 75% of the children are illegitimate and the way is paved for the cycle to repeat itself.'

'Aren't there unions to protect the wages?'

'Oh, yes. But the unions cannot raise wages without pricing the commodity out of the world market. Besides, if the labourer could save he would no longer be a labourer. He would start a small business and buy some land and earn enough to feed himself. There would not be enough to export and the standard of living would inevitably drop to his level.'

'Would he not consider marriage and a larger home?'

'Only as a status symbol on joining the middle class and on becoming a boss in his own right. The middle class is small and unstable, the ones on the way to 'bossdom' or on the way down to economic slavery. As a society this is doomed. Labour will only be necessary from the feeble-minded, the criminal, and the slave.'

'That is a long way away, don't be so serious. Let's dance and I will tell you about myself. What do you think of me?'

'I think that you are a spoilt child, running away from life. That you must be wealthy since you can afford to.'

'You are very direct. That must be because you are very introspective. Yet I am not as superficial as that. I have had a career and been divorced. I have been married and had a child. I have had my heavens and hells. Indeed, I have participated fully in life and I am now rich enough and content enough to be a spectator.'

'Have you a religion?'

'No standard one. I like churches and I believe in God. I am not presumptuous enough to believe He is interested in me or cares what I think about Him. I believe pain, misery, grief and remorse are natural ills to be overcome and that vice is over-indulgence in these ills. That virtue is the positive and healthy side of life and consists in the pursuit of happiness. Vice is hellish and virtue, heavenly.'

'That is good simple philosophy if you can afford it. As you say, it is only a spectator's philosophy.'

'Not really. I could convert you, but once again it is not necessary to do so. It is not my duty to do anything unless it gives me pleasure to do it.'

'What of the Ten Commandments? Could you kill, or steal, or covet another's husband?'

'All societies have their codes and these codes are enforced bylaws. If by stealing or killing I will end in jail, obviously I will refrain for that would not be a pleasant outcome. If my place in society is jeopardised by any action, and I cherish that place, then also I would refrain since once more the outcome would not be pleasant.'

'Would you let social sanctions determine your actions?'

'No. I do not need to, since society is a class system and I can choose my company and my class. Your labourer is curiously in a similar position since he cannot go any lower and has little chance of rising.'

'What happens when you acquire a husband?'

'I have already had one. Are you a only child?'

'Yes.'

'So was I, and my doting parents gave me a good education, made sure I travelled widely and finally, because I liked art, sent me to Paris to study art and dress designing. I became converted to Catholicism because it demanded so much and gave so much more. There is a serenity and a sense of inevitability mixed with knowledge that forgiveness is always possible. My parents were furious and denounced me. A fellow student befriended me, made me pregnant and persuaded me to marry him. I had six long months of hell while he persuaded me to give up my religion and make it up with my parents in order to inherit their money. My baby died and I decided that permanent security was better than occasional serenity. I wrote to my parents, gave up my religion, paid off my husband and divorced him. Any future husband will have to appreciate me as I am, with no illusions about changing me.'

'Will you continue this aimless life of continual holiday, from one hotel to another?'

'You are critical tonight. I can assure you that I am more useful in this world than you are. My investments and my business are being taken care of much more effectively in my absence and by interfering I can harm hundreds of people who depend on me for a living.'

'I am sorry, Janet. I did not mean to be so personal but we see so many kinds of tourists. If you look over at the bar you will see a couple of ladies in slacks and shirts. They are middle-aged, slightly drunk and on the lookout for local colour. If you overhear the conversation, it will nearly always be a titbit of news of nearly impossible behaviour of natives in different islands. They are quite happy to learn of lost Carib tribes, of child sacrifice and ritual abortions. Then one will go back to her hotel, trip over the mat, cut her head and vomit. This becomes an emergency and I will have to get out of bed to attend to her.'

'I see that you too have your prejudices, Peter.'

'I don't deny it. This place has a British culture and influence. All English virtues are emphasised: modesty, reserve, reverence for the queen and respect for civil service officials. Americans are criticised as brash, loud-mouthed and uncultured, with reverence only for cash. When I was a boy these differences were even more accentuated.'

'What was it like when you were a boy?'

'A little lonely, since I was not allowed out much. I spent most of my time on the estate with Dan and Clifton, and Lucille tagging along occasionally. The hotel life was also interesting, and I had a private tutor to prepare me for secondary school. There the days were more interesting. I was expected to be the leader and started off with a sense of superiority, but it took hard work and concentration to maintain the position. Dan and I were in the same class and he was slightly better, with much less effort. I wonder if he will come back this weekend.'

'What did he do?'

'He studied medicine by working nights and winning scholarships. He is now a lecturer in Washington.'

'And you have great regard for him?'

'He was my best friend and I have not seen him for more than ten years.'

'I hope you are not disappointed. You spend so much time worrying about the future and savouring its joys in anticipation that the present slips by unnoticed because it has not been planned. Life is a series of jolts in a world of dreams.'

'I must apologise again. The present is very pleasant. Let's dance and then go for a drive.'

'Hold on, let's us stick to the present and dance.'

Boy stood poised at the edge of the bay. It was a quiet spot and down below he could see the line of boys jostling at the water's edge, poised to dive. This was Saturday and they were waiting for the church bells to renew the hope of the world. He would dive and be cleansed. He had stripped off his bandages and was willing to die for God and for Pa. No one else seemed to think of his grandfather. Uncle Peter had come in to the hotel early this morning with that tourist woman. Pa was finished in everybody's mind. Christ too had been crucified yesterday – broken and beaten – but he was about to rise again in his tremendous triumph. Surely he would lift up Pa? Work another miracle if someone believed and prayed?

The joyful bells crashed out through the morning air, a score of lithe young bodies hit the water in one eager splash. He dived, clean and cleansed. His chest struck the surface. His body was wrapped in the warm shroud of water and in one effortless curve reached the bottom and arced up again to the surface. He lay on his back and watched the white clouds softly polish the blue dome of the sky for its hard midday glow. He had that feeling of exultation, of supreme self-sacrifice… his life for Pa's. Once more he wished that time would stop, that a moment could be projected and intensified, that it could be crystallised in to eternity.

He circled, turned and swam to the shore. His hands were sore as he pulled himself up on to the ledge, avoiding the long spikes of the black sea urchins. He sat on the ledge to dry.

Uncle Dan would come today. There had been a telegram this morning. He knew little about his uncle except the legends at school about his prowess at games and in class. He looked forward to his arrival as one who is terrified to be left alone.

He slipped on his shirt and shorts, picked up his shoes and

walked barefoot over the pebbly ground to the hotel.

The group walked down the track. Lent was over, the holidays were coming to an end and there were still so many things to be done to fill one's day. Catapults were there for the birds, mangoes to be sought. They could not exhaust the jokes about the teachers and friends, games and records, but they were looking for more activity. Boy did not see them coming until they turned the corner and were confronted. He would have preferred to avoid them but there was no way of doing that now.

'Hey! Look, the dream boy! What you carrying your shoes for? Your mammy can't buy you no more?'

Boy tried to keep on walking but the line blocked the track and he had to stop and look at Alphonse. The leader of a gang has his responsibilities. He must make the most of his opportunities to create interesting situations and Alphonse was only trying to provoke a situation by baiting. He and Boy had been great friends and had some respect for each other.

'Eh, eh! Hotel boys don't talk to us no more. I hear your Pa sick bad. What are you going to do when he dead?'

'Pa is not going to die.'

'Then why you swimming by yourself? Your father tell you not to play with us? You must choose your friends like your ma, nah?'

'Alphonse, get out of my way or you will regret it.'

'Hey, listen to him, man. He have big talk and fancy, fancy too.'

Boy tried to push his way past, but he was jostled from one to the other. Blindly he struck out and there was pain as his blistered fists landed. Then he was on the ground and they were laughing at him. He bit one, kicked another and then he was on his feet with a large stone in his hand. He charged and the line scattered. He kept on running past them, dropping the stone as he did so.

He reached the hotel and made for his room. Julie was cleaning it and was distressed to see the sobbing, dishevelled form, shoeless and with blood on his hands and face.

'Boy, Boy, what happen to you?'

'Alphonse and the boys were saying things about my mother.'

'Cha, you don't have to worry about those wharf rats. They have no training.'

'Alphonse is not a wharf rat. I beat them though. I wanted to kill them all.'

'Shush, Boy, don't talk so wild. Let me fix your hands before madam see them. She wouldn't like to know you fighting when your Pa dying.'

'Pa is not going to die, is he Julie?'

'I don't know that, Boy! That's for God to say.'

★

Lucille swept the house again and tidied up in expectation of Dan's arrival. She had stayed with her mother through the night and tried to persuade her to sleep. People kept dropping in to inquire about Clifton and to suggest various herbs and leaves and applications. Her mother insisted on staying awake in case Clifton awoke, and coffee was constantly percolating in the little metal container. The strong, small cups of coffee were offered to visitors and, with the soda biscuits from the tin, encouraged the visitors to stay and to converse in low respectful tones. It seemed that her mother was already practising for the wake. Lucille retired to a chair in the corner of the room and closed her eyes.

'Call me when you want to rest, Ma,' she said.

She slept fitfully, awakened by shuffling feet, barking dogs, cocks crowing and finally by her mother's hand on her shoulder. It was 5 a.m., and her mother wanted to go to early Mass. She washed her face and combed her hair while her mother put on her black hat and headed down to church. Lucille swept the house and prepared more coffee. The dogs under the house were whining. She wondered why they were not howling. Weren't dogs supposed to howl when someone was dying? She blew out the flame in the lamp and sat down beside her father. He breathed heavily through his mouth, the sounds becoming heavier and deeper, then ceasing for a while. His breathing seemed to tire him so that he had to pause regularly for rest.

Her mother returned with the dawn and asked whether he had moved.

'No, he's been just the same since you left.'

'He opened his eyes last night and asked for Dan.'

Lucille thought, you want to believe that and it does no harm.

Her mother had brought bread from the bakery and they breakfasted on bread and cocoa. The sunlight streamed through the trees and the visitors began again, mostly friends of her mother on their way to church or returning from church.

Then Boy came up a little after eight o'clock. He said Mrs Weston had received a telegram saying that Dan was arriving by plane that afternoon. He cast a wide-eyed look at the form on the bed and hurried away. Peter came in looking grim and professional. He looked tired and was almost brusque. He repeated his injection and turned to go.

'Isn't there anything I can do?' asked Lucille.

'He is dying, Lucille. All I can do is to try and keep him from suffering more than he has to.'

'Do you know that Dan is arriving today?'

'Good. Then you will have a second opinion. I will be back tonight.'

Clifton had woven all their lives in to an intricate pattern and with his dying it was beginning to fray.

Mrs Weston and Boy went to the airport to meet Daniel. Mrs Weston drove the hotel station wagon and they arrived at the long, low building ten minutes before the plane was due. It was near the end of the regular season and she was not expecting any guests. Boy was excited and drifted in and out of the groups of people who were waiting. He looked at the runway, the fire engines, the restaurant and the uniformed officials and airline personnel.

Mrs Weston checked that the plane was on time, found a chair and sat down. The distant hum became a roar and the plane swooped in out of the blue sky, touched down at the end of the runway, raced past the airport buildings, turned and came slowly back to the terminal. There was excited chatter as the gangway was wheeled to the door of the plane and brightly patterned frocks, large hats, elegant suits and wide smiles spilled down the steps towards the customs department. Daniel was one of the last of the passengers to leave the plane. She recognised him, although he did not resemble the boy who used to do odd jobs around the hotel. He seemed lean and hard and fit. Boy was jumping up and down excitedly beside her. Daniel glanced along the line of faces and waved as his eyes met hers. He moved on in to the building and she returned to her seat.

Boy stood looking in to the customs shed where Uncle Dan was greeting old school friends as he waited for his luggage. He missed nothing: the curious glances, the smile of welcome, the nod of recognition, the word of sympathy. Then Uncle Dan was striding out to the doorway. He ran to meet him.

'Uncle Dan!' Then shyness halted him and prevented him from looking up in to that lean brown face.

'Hello! Who are you?'

'I'm Boy!'

'Have you no name?'

'I am John... John Lawrence.'

'You must be Lucille's son. It's important to have a name, John. Where is Lucille?'

'She is at Pa's. Mrs Weston brought me.' Dan walked over to Mrs Weston.

'Thank you for coming for me. I expected Lucille.'

'She is helping your mother. Your father is badly burned and not expected to live. I will take you up now if you wish.'

'Do you mind if I stop at the hotel first and get cleaned up a little?'

'Not at all. Where will you stay while you are here?'

'At the hotel if you have a room.'

'I thought you would want to stay with your uncle.'

'I don't. Is there a room?'

'Why yes, Daniel, if you want one.'

They climbed in to the front seat of the station wagon and Boy could sense the icy prickles of arrogance and anger from Mrs Weston. She was thinking how ungrateful people were and deciding to take no more cheek. In the meantime, silence would put him in his place.

'Who is Pa's doctor, Mrs Weston?'

'My son, Peter.'

'Oh Peter! I'll have a chat with him after I see Pa.'

'I expect you will.'

The silence settled thickly between them and the car snapped in to low gear to grind up the steep slope to the hotel.

Still a bitch, thought Daniel, *and a determined one too, I bet.*

Boy sat uncomfortably between them, absorbing the waves of antipathy. Dan sat back and looked over the landscape, noting all the changes and feeling the odd strangeness of renewed familiarity... the feeling that one knows all this and should be able to tell what lies round the next corner but cannot quite recall it... a teasing déjà vu quality.

They pulled up with a jerk at the entrance of the hotel and Dan and Boy piled up the suitcases. She turned to Dan.

'I'm sorry about your father. Boy will show you your room. If there is anything I can do, please let me know.'

'Thank you, Mrs Weston.'

Boy lay on the grass near the edge of the cliff and looked down at the bay and the town across the bay. The wind waved through the grass and whispered, but it was a language he did not know. He watched the boats in the bay. Uncle Peter had a boat. It was a twenty-two-foot sloop with a small cabin, and he had gone sailing with him a few times. It was fun to sail. The boat heeling over, going hard in to the wind and the bow cleaving through the water. He remembered the last sail.

'You love sailing, don't you, John?'

'Yes, Uncle Peter, I do.'

'Would you want to be a sailor when you grow up?'

'No, I don't think so. I would not want to be on those iron ships.'

'What would you like to be?'

'I think I should like to be a priest.'

'A priest! Why?'

'I am not sure but I cannot think of anything else I would like to do.'

'There are many professions in the world and you do not see many kinds on this small island, so I can see why it is difficult for you to decide. You are young and you have plenty of time to make up your mind.'

'I thought of being a librarian so that I would never run out of books to read.'

'That is not a bad second choice. I hope you are going to study and go to university, because there can be a lot of excitement in life.'

'I know that, but I remember when I made my first communion. I wished I could die and go to Heaven right away.'

'That is a very morbid thought. To be one of the chosen, one must first be tried in the fire of life.'

'The priest says I just have to be in a state of grace.'

'Of course. I was only teasing you. Don't you want to be a pilot and fly through the air in a big aeroplane? You don't have to do something that keeps you on the island. It can be fun and exciting to travel.'

'Can I steer the boat for a while?'

'Certainly! You are here to watch the jib and keep it filled. If it starts fluttering you are going up too much.'

It was exciting and he managed well enough.

Boy wondered what he would really like to be. A bird to fly around and glide in the currents of the wind? No! It would be better to be the wind stirring the treetops, bringing the rain, pushing the sails and moving the restless clouds: soothing, gentle, roaring, threatening, destructive wind.

Dan was not certain why he had returned. Perhaps it was the accidental nature of his father's injury or an idea that he might be able to help. Now he stood in his hotel room preparing for this meeting with his father. Neither of his parents had been demonstrative people. His father had always shown more interest in Peter Weston than himself. His mother's only interest had been his father's comfort. Lucille was the only real tie in the family. The little sister he had loved and scolded, beaten and protected.

He left his room to meet John in the reception room and together they began the walk to his childhood home. There was no point in questioning John about his life. A pity that a child is too inarticulate to express the wonders and intense emotions he feels on being exposed to life changes. So many experiences still had this quality of newness at that age, and adult's reactions were the least comprehensible.

This walk was familiar, for he had walked up and down with Peter hundreds of times from childhood to manhood, in joy and grief, in pride and despair. Why was he walking it again? The good got out, the fools remained. That was the pattern of island life. It was for a short time and, having seen his father, he would leave. He would not be trapped by sentiment, by any idea of belonging, of owing and repaying. The pattern was too tightly woven. The inferiority cult, reinforced by books, by idiom, public school and the class system, and every so often a little riot, revolt or war to put down. There was nothing to be gained by fighting it oneself in a small corner.

His father had never fought it. As a member of the Volunteer Reserves he had helped stop more than one riot. A solid second-class citizen! He had worshipped his father as a boy, striven for his love and affection, then gradually hated him when all his sacrifices had proved vain. Yet there was no doubt about the driving force in his life and he ought to be grateful.

The little house was even smaller than he remembered it. He walked up the step and was recognised by Lucille, who called out.

'Ma! Here's Dan.'

There was no effusive welcome from Lucille. His mother came out and welcomed him, then led him in to the bedroom. He was unprepared for what he saw. He was used to hospital conditions, and the sick and the dying did not distress him. This man was dying, but he was dying in a small room with serum leaking through his dressings and pyjamas.

He turned away from the man and beckoned Lucille.

'Let's go for a walk. I would like to talk to you.'

They walked under the trees as they had done more than ten years ago. Life had been a game to be played and enjoyed. Now there were so many barriers and secrets between them.

'Lucille, everything seems so strange. Can you tell me a little of all that has happened?'

'You mean about Boy and Peter and Pa?'

'Yes, and about yourself.'

Once again she went over the old story of ambition and failure, seduction, pride and shame.

'I left home and went to live at Uncle Randolph's. This was after Pa stopped Peter from marrying me. I worked on the roads until the election came. Peter was one of the candidates and Uncle Randolph tried to persuade Pa to oppose him. Peter would have got in if Randolph had not opposed him himself. They made it a family issue and I spoke on the platform. I wanted revenge more than anything else.'

'And now Pa is dying. What will you do?'

'I don't know. I haven't thought about it.'

'You must take John and come to the States. There is a future there for both of you. There is nothing here but traditional futility. You have wasted so much of your life already fighting it. Even if you won there would be no merit gained. Tell Ma I'll be back later.'

He took a short cut through the trees to avoid the house and made his way back to the hotel. The receptionist told him Peter was in the lounge waiting for him. He walked in and saw Peter sitting in an armchair and chatting to a pretty red-haired girl. The girl noticed him and said something to Peter, who looked round and jumped to his feet.

'Hello, Dan, I'm pleased to see you back, although I'm sorry about the condition causing your return.'

Janet said, 'Excuse me. I'll leave you two boys to your chat.'

'Oh, Dan, this is Janet. Janet, this is Dr Daniel Lawrence.'

'Pleased to meet you. Excuse me now. I'll be back later.'

They shook hands and sat down as she walked away.

'Not bad, Peter, you're not as shy as you used to be.'

'No, she's a nice girl and easy to talk to.'

'I've seen Lucille and she tells me you've had a shot at elections as well.'

'Yes, but no success. I suppose you saw Clifton. What do you think of him?'

'Nothing can be done now. Why couldn't something be done before?'

'Like what, Dan?'

'Hospital? Intravenous fluids? Full resuscitation?'

'Do you know the hospital? No, of course not. I'll take you round tomorrow. It's a cottage hospital, casualties, mainly emergencies and nursing care. Even with the best possible care the chances were heavily against your father.'

'I know, but with no care there was no chance.'

'There was no point in instituting treatment which could not be carried out properly and had no chance of affecting the outcome.'

'What ever *can* be treated if this defeatist attitude is shared by all the doctors here? Your patients are those who would recover anyway or who would have a good chance of doing so with or without treatment!'

'I'm sorry, Dan, but I did not create the conditions. I've found them so and I've tried to improve them but there is more than enough work as it is now. The relief of pain and anxiety, the reassurance to relatives of a doctor's presence – these may seem minimal duties to you but they are important.'

'These are the functions of the obeah man and the social welfare worker and the nurse. Medicine is a science. How can you be satisfied to ignore this?'

'I don't. My knowledge of the science is kept up to date and used when necessary, but medicine is partly an art. The science part is becoming more extensive but also it is being taken over by machines and computers and that is all to the good. We will have gone the full cycle with the art of medicine being the only part left to the doctor, apart from the craftsmanship of the surgeon.'

'All this is true, but meanwhile don't you feel reproached when someone dies who could have been saved by even a moderate amount of care?'

'Of course I do, but that does not mean I should pull up and go where conditions are better. Someone had to be here doing this work and the keener his interest, the better his work. Your father could not be saved by a moderate amount of care. It would require intensive care facilities and even with those the chances would be small.'

'The work is quite limited, as you have pointed out. Could you not leave it to others who can cope equally well under these conditions? A good nurse could work as effectively.'

'You are a prouder man than I am and perhaps you have just cause to be, but I am content to be a good nurse most of the time, if at all times I remain a good doctor.'

'Most serious arguments about conditions, Peter, end up by agreeing to differ and there is no point arguing further.'

'Don't run away, Dan. Instead of criticising, why don't you give up your big practice and come down to show us how to raise the standards here.'

'Why? This place is backward. It can serve but two purposes. Tourism – "See the isles of paradise and the enchanted slaves." But beware! For it is also a spawning ghetto – cheap labour raised at little cost. Tighten your immigration laws and produce your automation.'

Peter looked up to see his father approaching. Daniel stood up to greet him.

'Daniel, I am pleased to see you back here with us. How is your father doing?'

They shook hands and Daniel replied, 'Very poorly. There is not much more that can be done for him.'

'Pity that medical science does not have the answer to everything.'

Dan looked at Peter.

'It is, but medical science cannot be held responsible in this case. More could have been done in this case if facilities had been available. It appears that you cannot afford it.'

'I hope you will be staying here to practise.'

'No, thanks. There would be no future in that. I have been trying to persuade Peter to make better use of his skills and knowledge by working where better facilities are available. I feel strongly about this, that one should make full use of one's skill. Perhaps it is not so important for a European to do so.'

'That is an odd statement,' said Peter. 'What has race got to do with it?'

'Everything. The European does not have to prove how clever he is. Look around and you will see the print of his works. The non-European has not had a chance to catch up, and the Negro particularly has to prove he can do it.'

'The Japanese seem to be doing very well,' said Frank.

"Yes, they were quick to realise that it is necessary to outdo the West in order to keep up with it.'

'Why is it necessary to westernise? Why can't a nation retain its cultural identity and work out its own solutions?' asked Peter.

'Because the world is too small; because the means of communication are controlled by the West; because the West is coming closer together in a union, economic and military, while her former colonies are drifting around. They have her culture and her religion, both of which are disadvantages. What they need are her science and her technology, otherwise they are doomed.'

'What is wrong with Christianity?' asked Peter.

'Nothing,' said Dan, 'except that it appears to be only for export and foreign consumption. I would have a lot more faith in it if, in countries where segregation reigns, minorities were taught in colleges and seminaries where races are mixed, if these ministers preached to mixed congregations and did not enter churches, halls and schools where these basic Christian ideas were not entertained. Christianity is disappointing because one expects so much of Christians. Perhaps it is no longer a suitable religion for Europeans when wealth, domination and self-advancement have become most important. Yet it is shameful when it is used as a tool to bribe the underprivileged.'

'You know,' Frank said, 'Peter will find it hard to argue with you because he has a guilt complex. I am not sure why, but I feel it is due to a poor basic education. I should have sent him abroad to public school as his mother suggested. However, I can answer your arguments. There is no western plot as you see it. We have had two great wars between western powers. At the moment Russia and half of Europe, which are western nations, are busy fighting an ideological war with the rest of the West. As individuals, we all struggle for more and more comfort and more material advantages. We do not try to convert others, we leave that to those who offer spiritual comfort. If my property ceases to be profitable, then I will try to disguise the fact and sell it for as much as I can to someone else. The race of that someone else will not be important. The struggle is purely materialistic and you have to compete. As the world becomes smaller, then you have no choice about competing, whatever your ambitions. There is no hope of a union of other races. An American Negro is more American than Negro; the Chinese do not like Indians and the Indians love the Westerners. If you are hoping for an east/west or black/white conflict you will be disappointed.'

'You may be right, Mr Weston, and I am not hoping for a conflict, although history would be on the side of the barbarians being successful against civilisation. I am worried about the change in the nature of production. Your system of production will be unable to compete against mechanical systems, and as machines replace labour while reproduction rates increase, there'll be an enormous glut of unemployable labour. Which races will suffer first? You state that the struggle for existence is purely a class struggle, a materialistic one, but then the Jews do not find it so. There is a need to identify oneself in a family and a nation as a group. The colour of skins is a very definite means of identification. International groups whose purpose has been to control the actions of individual nations have always failed, and will always fail, because the representative man is even more human than the individual man. The great failing of man is that he is basically selfish and will only act in his own interest. Tell me, Peter, if a medical congress were asked to legalise abortions and sterilisation in a planned campaign in the future, have you any doubt which of the races would suffer the most, supposing these recommendations could be enforced?'

'That is a question, Dan, that I cannot answer, because the question is unlikely to arise, and if it did, then a scientific answer would be sought from your computers, but your computers can also be biased by the programming. Dad was suggesting that I have a guilt complex and you also share that opinion simply because I refuse to see race as an insuperable barrier to world peace. Perhaps, as Dad suggests, it is because I was born and educated here. It is not only the black colonial who is a second-class citizen. The white colonial is also exposed to the same off-hand treatment and is impressed with the idea of being an ungrateful, parasitic nuisance holding on to magnificent host. The difference is that, on reaching the mother country, he can be absorbed and become indistinguishable from a first-class citizen.'

'Peter, to know that there is a way out must be pleasant.'

'All this,' said Frank, 'sounds very much like an inferiority complex.'

'Not a complex, Mr Weston, it is a cult, a deliberate cultivating of satellite states, which is necessary if a minority group is going to hold power over a wide area indefinitely. One cannot afford to encourage development in a major group and still control it, unless of course it is genuinely inferior.'

'Anyway, Daniel, please make yourself at home but don't start any revolution. If you make any takeover bids I am willing to sell out to you… at the right price of course!'

Peter smiled at Daniel.

'Dan, you can borrow my car for the afternoon if you want to, and take Boy with you.'

After Daniel had left, Frank Weston continued talking to Peter.

'Someday you have to run the hotel, the business and the estate.'

'I suppose so, but that is still a long time away, I hope.'

'I am the same age as Clifton and he is dying. I remember when I first returned after my university days, I wasn't sure I wanted any part of it either. I was born here and my father ran the biggest business in town – dry goods, hardware and groceries.

'I had been away since I was eight and I had spent my time at boarding school and university. Most years I came home by boat for the long summer holidays but towards the end I returned less frequently. My mother had died when I was very young and there were no brothers and sisters to keep me company when I came home, all my friends were those I had made abroad. So I studied economics and got married after finishing my exams. I had a good allowance, and your mother and I travelled around Europe. She became pregnant and we returned to England where you were born.

'At that stage I decided it was time to come home, and my father had been hinting about this for a long time. Once more we travelled leisurely by boat and when we arrived we found that my father had not made any plans about where we would stay. Joan has never liked this place so I looked around and found an estate for sale, bought it and built my home. I wasn't interested in the store then either. My father suggested that I could work for the Palmers, who had the big sugar estates, so that I could learn something about management. I did their accounts for them. I often had to go to the factory to discuss wages and production and the number of employees. So I was there that August when the riots broke out.

'Someone noticed that there was a fire in the fields and then we heard loud shouts and excited chatter. We saw some people running in from the fields. These were the overseers and they were tired and frightened. They said the men had stopped work and were marching on the factory. I suppose if I had the car I might have driven away. In those days you were lucky to have one car per family, and Joan had driven me down and arranged to come back about four o'clock. The factory people were the engineers, the manager, myself, two foremen and the stokers. The manager complained that he had a revolver but no one else was armed. I pointed out that this was probably a good thing because we would have a short battle, and bloodshed ending in burning the factory.

'The shouting crowd of people came nearer and they were led by Randolph Lawrence. I have never understood why no one has shortened that name to Randy. He waved both arms above his head and the mob quietened down. He shouted to the manager that they were closing the factory and marching to town. The manager replied that they were crazy and brought out his revolver.

' "If I shoot you, all these men will run away," he said.

' "You fool, you want them to kill and burn?" said Randolph.

'The mob waved their cutlasses and began to surge forward. "No! We are not starting that," said Randolph, and he walked towards the manager. I could see the manager's shaking hand and was certain he would fire. Randolph reached out and took hold of the gun. He did not pull at it. He said "Give it to me!" and the manager released it. Then Randolph stepped forward and slapped him across the face. The crowd cheered. I doubt I have ever seen a more tense or dramatic moment. Afterwards, we were herded in to the factory, the doors were closed and we were shut in. It was late evening before we were released by people from the town.

'I decided I had had enough of dealing with raw labour and advised my father not to consider buying the sugar estates. I joined him in the business and grew cocoa, coconuts and citrus on my estates and I have done so ever since. The war years came along and some of the younger, unmarried men went off to war. Otherwise it did not affect us very much. You were young then and we could not send you away to boarding school for primary or secondary education. After the war you went away to university to study. After my father died, and I built the hotel.

'*Now* you are a doctor and aspire to be a politician. When I need help with my business! At some time you will have to run it. I hope you do not leave it too late. If it is power you want, there is more power in expanding the companies to real estate, to construction, to starting a bank. In that direction lies power, much more than in making speeches and begging help from other nations. Please think about it seriously. You are not so young anymore and neither am I. I must know whether you are interested before deciding to go on.'

Peter reflected, 'You can count on me to help where it is necessary and when it is essential. Since I have no experience in business it is no use asking me to organise anything. If I am made a director of one or more of your companies perhaps I can begin to understand how they work.'

'Very well! We will leave it like that at the moment.'

Boy was sitting in one of his caves. Today was an underground as opposed to a space day, and he was using his vast system of subterranean communication to confound Britain's navies. It was an interesting system of transport, with jet trains in those tunnels, and most difficult for the enemies to detect. Even the advanced nations were puzzled, and the stupid primitive tribes never realised how their plans were so quickly discovered. There had been a little trouble in the Zambesi. Charles and himself had put that right. Charles was his English friend to whom he had shown the secrets of the cave. Boy still felt a little squeamish about the slaughter. The poor native warriors with spears and leather shields had rushed to their machine gun outpost. They looked really ferocious in their warpaint and ringed noses. He could hear their blood-curdling yells even now.

Poor fools! They did not stand a chance and had been slain in their hundreds. He had felt it was unfair to fight spears with machine guns but Charles had no time for his squeamishness. Were they not heavily outnumbered? Could they afford to lose and let down the side? And lastly, it was no use having superior weapons if you did not use them. All of which sounded sensible to Boy. However, he was glad that on this occasion they had not carried atomic warheads.

Far off he heard his name being called. He looked cautiously out of the cave. There were no enemies in sight. He slipped out and ran swiftly up to the hotel.

Dan took Boy for a drive that afternoon, past the abandoned airport which had once been a coconut plantation. Through the wooden villages with fruit stalls of water melon, pineapples and mangoes where wandered ragged children with large bellies and big smiles. Dan pondered on the dangers of malnutrition, the accepted hazard 80% of the population had to face in the first two years of life and the cause of half the deaths in the community. This was survival of the fittest of course, but how fit were the survivors? Next would come the trial by worms and then the trial by education, before being relegated to the scrapheap of labour.

'Boy, do you like school?'

'It's all right, Uncle Dan.'

'Do you get a lot of homework?'

'No, we don't have homework.'

'Do you have any books to study from?'

'Oh yes, we have readers, and arithmetic and grammar books.' Boy was puzzled for a moment. 'It's a good thing we have, because with all the noise and the boys between me and the blackboard, I wouldn't learn much in class.'

'Do you ever run away from school?'

Boy flushed and the shadow of the headmaster blotted out the sunlight filtering in through the window of the school.

'No, I got beaten once for that.'

'Do you like being here?'

'I don't know.'

'Would you like to live in America?'

'Oh yes! Skyscrapers and cowboys and trains. It would be exciting.'

'Don't you like swimming, sailing, fishing, football, scouts and climbing trees?'

'Yes, Uncle Dan. It's fun when you have lots of friends.'

Dan drove down by the stretch of beach and stopped the car. This could be so pleasant to retire to –warm and pleasant. One had but to shed one's responsibility.

'Do you know this beach, John?'

'Yes, Uncle Dan. The hotel car brings the guests down here every Sunday.'

'Well, let's go and see Uncle Randolph.'

Dan drove back to town following Boy's instructions and stopped at Randolph Lawrence's door. It was a wooden, two-storey building with garage, kitchen and servant's quarters downstairs. Boy had not been to his uncle's house before but he knew it, and he also knew that his mother lived there. They went upstairs and were met by Randolph, who was delighted to see Dan.

'Come in, man! I'm sorry about Clifton, but I am pleased to see you. I hear that you have been doing well for yourself. I hope that you are going to stay.'

'No, Uncle Randolph, not me. I called to have a little chat with you. I hear that you are doing well yourself.'

'Well, I am a businessman and we won the last elections. Yes, I suppose I am quite comfortable, thank you. All over the world, people fight and compete, work and slave, put aside ideas of humanity and comfort in order to retire to a place like this. The few who do make it have only one regret, that they are not a little younger than retirement age. What do you want of life?'

'I want success and fame. I want to inspire others by my example. I want my race proud of me.'

'You are a dreamer, but make sure that you know what you want. You can have success and fame without inspiring others or causing any other emotion than envy. This is a western world, practical and hard, and success is measured in cash. I am a success and your father is not. The difference between us is that I fought and won. Your father could also have fought and he would have won because he has much more ability than I, but he decided that to fight was disloyal and wrong. He was confused as to whom he owed loyalty. His light was not only hidden under a bushel, it was put out by himself lest it offend by its brightness.'

'My father—'

'I know he was good and kind and never knowingly hurt anyone in his life. That is why you ran away to assert yourself. That is why Lucille has been fighting and getting hurt. You want to be a martyr to race, as he has been, but you feel his passive resistance has failed. Believe me, you will achieve more by aiming at a definite target and as an individual expecting help from no one.'

'Like crabs in a barrel, Uncle?'

'You have been steeped in propaganda. Let me tell you more about your father. He never left this island. I did, and I never saw anyone sell anything by advertising its faults. I saw beggars in all countries and I saw Indian princes and African chiefs claiming respect in all countries while their countrymen starved. It is difficult to read a moral in to this story, except that it does not pay to be at the bottom of the barrel. I have done more for this place than your father did.'

'What have you done, and what can you do in a place like this? You have no raw materials and you have only labour to offer. Since slavery is abolished you cannot sell that. You can sell the sunny beaches and the choppy waters and the unspoiled countryside to tourists until enough of them settle down. Then the countryside will no longer be unspoiled, the sunny beaches will have been sold and you will have to pay by the hour to listen to the lapping waters.'

'If that is progress, Daniel, I will accept it. In the meantime I can improve the standard of living by making certain that money is spent here and remains here, and all this buying and selling is not transacted in a distant country. I now help to shape the policies.'

'Don't you think that government will now discriminate against Europeans, here and in other places that are becoming independent?'

'You would like them to, wouldn't you, Dan? America breeds more race hatred than these islands. What would be the purpose of discriminating? In the world of management and business it pays to choose the best workers, regardless of colour. Where it is a question of charity, then obviously charity begins at home. Eventually, with greater experience and training, the majority of all jobs, the best included, will belong to the majority group. If an apartheid arrangement develops then it should be a voluntary one, not imposed by government.'

'Randolph, while you are struggling to be fair, you forget that in Europe it is necessary for your men to be superior to be considered equal.'

'Dan, that is what I have been trying to say. Man is an individual and he has arranged society for his own benefit, not society's. I am superior to you until you prove your superiority to me, and then I will consider you my equal.'

'OK, Uncle, I will still try to paint a broader canvas because I feel the majority is average, and the average is stupid, easily influenced and too well steeped in prejudice to be reclaimed.

What do you suggest that Lucille should do?'

'Have you spoken to her?'

'Oh yes, I have asked her to return to the States with me.'

'Did she agree?'

'Not yet, but I think she will.'

'I hope she does not interfere with your plans over there.'

'No. She can earn her own living and get married.'

'What about you? Won't you get married?'

'Not for a while. I chose medicine to be free to move about and shape my destiny. Marriage at the moment would be a tie. You, Uncle, should be married and add to your comfort.'

'I may consider it soon but I have been too busy before. We have shaky morals in this island and I have been no saint.'

Boy stood listening to this conversation between his uncles. He was looking out of the window across the harbour. There was a tourist ship alongside one of the docks, and the taxis were wheeling like vultures to approach the dock and pick up the passengers. He could see the gesticulations of the drivers and could almost hear the shouts and protests across the hump of the town. The actions were threats even at this distance, like looking through the schoolroom windows at the bright cruelty of the sunshine.

He preferred the rain pounding on the tin rooftops and slashing across the concrete playground when the gusts slammed at the doors and windows. There was the cool comfort of the dark when the windows and doors were shut, and the steady drumming of the rain on the walls and roof. There was the shouting excitement as one tried to be heard above the noise of everything else. The thunder and the flashing lightning generated an electric potential in the crowd. Then came the sweaty smell of five hundred people in one closed room and the freshness of the air as doors and windows were opened. Once he remembered sitting in class when…

'What is potash? Lawrence, wake up! What is potash?' There was a nudge and he scrambled to his feet.

'Well, Lawrence,' the teacher was saying, 'What is potash? A penny if you know and twelve lashes if you don't.'

The teacher was gambling on his educational system. No one

was interested in agriculture as a subject. It had to be taught since the 'back to the land' movement had begun. *Potash,* he thought, *something burnt out, gone to pot.* It was obvious but the obvious answers were never correct. He shivered in anticipation. The threat of physical violence always unnerved him.

'A mineral salt,' he heard the prompter beside him whisper. His dry mouth could hardly shape the words. He stuttered to the amusement of the class.

'Yes, yes. Where is it found Lawrence?'

There was again the tightening in the pit of the stomach. He guessed wildly: it has to do with agriculture… in plants and soil, sir.' The teacher was still suspicious.

'All right, Lawrence, sit down and pay attention.'

'Yes, sir.'

He was thankful he had not disgraced himself and wet his pants. You got laughed at for that. Strange to say, he got his penny after class had been dismissed.

He wished he could have shared the coconut cake he bought with his prompter, but he was not allowed to be friendly with Ralph because he was Uncle Randolph's illegitimate son.

'John, would you like some lemonade?' Uncle Randolph came over to the window. 'What are you looking at?'

He looked out at the sunset over the harbour.

'That big tourist ship over there, Uncle, I wonder where it is going to next?'

'Would you like some lemonade?'

'Yes, please.'

'Go and tell the maid we want two whiskeys and sodas, and a lemonade. She has not been doing much since Lucille left.'

When John returned, he listened to his uncle talking to Daniel.

'It was a strange world but then all worlds including this one we live in are strange. For those of us who lived in that world, it was the only one there was. We lived in the large town but we knew of others which were smaller because, being fishermen, we did travel to other towns to coves and beaches where there were only a few people. Most of us were fishermen most of the time. The only other occupation was working the land, and the seasonal employment of cutting cane at harvest time. There were richer people around but those were few. They worked for government or were merchants or owned large estates. Then there were the priests, because in those days most people went to church on Sundays and other days as well. The Church gave some meaning, some purpose, some drama to existence. It also provided the only education there was. Both primary and secondary school were the work of the Church. Government only governed.

'There were few good roads, except to the estates, and cars were very few. There was no electricity, but in the main town there were gas lights in the streets and lamp lighters employed by the town council went around in the evenings to light them. The rest of us used candles, kerosene lamps and gas lights. Food had to be fresh or salted or tinned. Even government was simple and set apart. There was a king, far away, who sent a governor and administrator, who appointed civil servants. There was a legislative council made up of a few appointed by the governor and a few elected by larger land owners and merchants. So, you see, we were grateful to the priests who assured us that we were loved by God and that we were all equal in His sight, despite everything. We tried to benefit from the education they provided but most of us could have only some primary school education and become the lower ranks of civil servants. The top posts in the civil service were filled by people imported by government.

'There was no TV, and not even radio, except for a few which were battery operated. There was a daily newspaper which told us all we needed to know about ourselves and the rest of the world.

'There were few professionals, two or three doctors, two or three lawyers, two magistrates and an occasional judge. There was one little hospital to which we took our very sick. Since there were no roads and no ambulances, these were carried in hammocks slung on one stout pole and carried by two people.

'We knew that our island was not the only one in the world because we did have schooners that traded from island to island and occasionally a large steamer would come from the outside world, and the wireless provided news which our paper printed for us.

'I tell you all this so that you will know the country in which my brother and I grew up. He was three years older than I was, and I was always jealous of the fact that he was bigger and stronger and doing things I could not yet do. He went to school earlier, he finished earlier and he went fishing earlier. In the end this all evened out because I finished school in sixth standard and I too could not afford secondary school, so I too went fishing. It was hard work so I had no reason to be jealous. We went out late afternoon, rain or shine, and fished from an open boat with the aid of a lantern all through the night. No one would do this for fun because we had to find fish to survive. We had to go far out to sea in all kinds of weather and all kinds of waves and wind, and we had to row back long distances when the wind was not favourable. It was lonely work.

'Sometimes there was nothing to be seen but troubled seas. Foaming white caps and nothing to hear but the sound of the breaking waves. On clear nights there were the stars or the moon, and dawn would show where the east was.

'Alternative employment was cutting cane, and this was preferable even though it was also hard work. There were lots of people, loud chatter, jokes and laughter. There was the sight of the mules pulling the empty wagons back for us to fill. They ran head high, neck outstretched, ears back against the head, legs lifting high to avoid the wooden beams, supporting the rails, their side dark and shining with sweat. They rested while the wagons were being loaded and ran back again to be unloaded at the factory.

'Our father became too old to work in the cane fields but he continued to fish, and that is why we were not with him that August when we were cutting cane and he went out to sea. He should have read the signs because it was a still, hot day and the wind, what little there was, had shifted to the west. He went out with two other fishermen, and during the night the wind came up and roared through the trees and the houses. It flattened the canes, it tore off large branches and knocked down some trees. Some roofs came flying off and houses shook. The waves got higher and higher. Wives and mothers worried all night about their families at sea. Our father and his two companions never returned and our mother would not let us go back to sea again.

Conflict

That was thirty years ago... before you were born.

'Your father and I were seeing the same girl. He married her and decided to become a policeman, and I joined a schooner and travelled up and down the islands. That was 1928, and the following year all the problems began in the States, with the Great Depression and people jumping out of windows. Things remained much the same here. You were born and your father became a sergeant in the police force. However, conditions were changing in all the islands. The price of sugar was going down. Wages remained the same but the price of imported goods was going up, and life was becoming harder for everyone. Discontent was in the air and people were beginning to ask questions. A man named Walker returned with me to St. Lucia. He had been sent to start a trade union. He spoke to the workers in the village and I joined him and spoke as well. The council and the administration were alarmed and they deported Walker. I become the leader and founder of the union. Meanwhile, your father had become a sergeant major in the police force and that was as high as he could go.'

The maid came in with the tray on which stood the decanter of whisky, a soda siphon and two glasses.

'Thank you! Did you give John his lemonade? I am sure he would like another. John, go and get another lemonade.'

After John had left Randolph continued his story, 'Electricity had come to the island and with it more radios. There were also more boats calling in, because it was a good harbour and it was a coaling station. We even had a seaplane land in the harbour – a De Havilland, I believe. We were becoming modernised and the roads were improved; some tourists began to walk the streets. Salvation Army bands played and roamed the same streets. It was a time of change.

'For the first time, men began to emigrate: to Panama to work on the land, to French Guyana, to Cayenne to work and look for gold, and, finally, even to the United States. There were those who could not leave and conditions were becoming worse. The trade union demanded increased wages for workers. The employers refused. The trade union asked the men to demonstrate and threatened to strike. The employers knew that the strike would fail because there were many more men, maybe older, maybe less fit, but still, workers who would take their place. So they began to dismiss the troublemakers and replace them.

'I used to have long conversations with my brother. Chance had led us different ways and it now began to look like opposite ways. "Why are you doing this?" he would say.

' "Because you no longer can take advantage of us!"

' "How am I taking advantage of you?"

' "You are supporting the foreigners who are abusing the workers."

' "They are giving employment, wages to live on. Have you forgotten that you too once worked for them?"

' "I have not forgotten. I was younger then and I could buy more with those wages than they can buy now. All we are asking is a little more pay."

' "Let's forget who is right and who is wrong. What happens when they say no, when they tell you they cannot give any more?"

' "Then we march and we ask the governor to make them give us more."

' "And then the governor says no. What do you do?"

' "Then we fight."

' "You fight? We have machine guns that can tear you in to pieces. All you have is cutlass and stick."

' "Then we retreat and we wait for you to sleep and we cut your heads off. We work in silence."

' "What then? Who going pay you? Who going to govern you? You will have anarchy. No law, no nothing."

' "Oh! My brother! They have taken your mind as well as your body. We can govern ourselves! We can work the land. We are not children who must be looked after always. We have grown up!"

' "Then the king will send more soldiers and destroy you. Do you think he can allow this in one of his lands? Do you think he can let you do this and not be punished? Do you think he can forgive you? Do you think he is God?"

'That was not the full conversation but a summary of various conversations. I also tried to enlist him and his policemen, since he was virtually the chief. The inspector was a foreigner and would not be expected to relate to his staff. If I had him and his police with me I could have the whole island with me, no trouble. So I said to him, "You could save everyone time and trouble if you and your police sided with me." He was horrified.

' "We have sworn an oath to be loyal to the government and the king, to support the law, and you ask me not only that I break my oath but that I ask others to do so. Further, I hope you realise that I will now be suspect, as your brother, of collaborating with you whether I do or not. So you are causing me enough trouble already."

' "Well! Then you will have to do your work while I do mine."

'We had organised a regular trade union and had twelve officers and a chain of command. We demanded negotiations and got them, but they broke down since no agreement could be reached. We asked for the intervention of the governor and gave notice of strike. We pulled the men from the fields, got them off the mule trains and closed the factories. Some fires were started in the cane fields but we discouraged this action and arranged a march to Government House. There was no ugly mood. In fact, we were singing folk songs and waving cutlasses and sticks.

'News had spread to the capital and my brother took a detachment of policemen to Government House and left the rest of the police in the police station. Everyone could hear us from miles away because we were shouting, laughing and singing. People lined the road to watch and some joined us. We reached Government House and the metal gates were shut and behind them the policemen lined up in ranks armed with rifles. We demanded an interview with the governor. You know, that was an opportunity for the governor to meet all the ringleaders, but he refused.

'The crowd got restless and began to rattle the gates, and all it needed was a surge forward. Your father ordered them to stop or he would shoot. He ordered the police to fire over the heads of the crowd. A volley rang out and there was confusion and screaming as people scattered. Many were injured by being trampled on and one man had been shot.

'I was told that he had been standing beside me. I was dragged away by others. I shouted to them and got some order and we began to march in to the town. There were no policemen there.

We broke windows, rattled doors and threw stones. We did little damage for an angry mob but we did cause fear and consternation. The men scattered through the streets and after many hours they all made their way back to their homes.

'The strike dragged on and the factories remained closed but there was a warrant out for my arrest for inciting a riot. I remained hidden in the country in the homes of friends. One day my brother came and urged me to leave the country.

' "You cannot hide on this island. It is much too small and too many people talk. I made it my business to reach you before the others do."

'I was smuggled aboard a coaling ship and stowed away. I had my passport, so in Liverpool I jumped ship and joined the Merchant Navy. I spent the war years in the Merchant Navy and returned to the island at the end of the war.

'By that time many people had jumped on the bandwagon and were claiming to be the leaders of the revolution. The political climate was different and we agitated for universal suffrage and got it. You know the rest of the story.

'What you do not know was that after I left the island, pressure was brought on your father to resign. He did that and took up his present job. We have had little to say to each other since, but he did come to me to help pay your way while you were at university.'

'I am grateful for your help.'

'That was not the point. What I am saying is that between Clifton and me there has been little friendship or conversation, and that many people believe we are mortal enemies. They speculate whether it is about your mother or the police work, but no one is certain. It is simply that we drifted so far apart and it was up to me to make the first moves to heal the wounds. Now there is no time left to do so.'

'He knows that you looked after Lucille when she needed help. It would have been better if you two had remained as close as family ought to be, but my father was always proud and independent and it would have been difficult for him to make the first move. I needed to know the whole story and there are still a couple of points I am not clear about. You make it sound purely chance that you went one way and Clifton the other.'

'Yes, he married Sarah and assumed responsibility for a family while I accepted responsibility for the society or perhaps only the working section. At first, marriage does tend to be self limiting, especially when children come along. Perhaps you should blame yourself.'

'I am not attempting to blame anyone. I am merely looking for causes. He probably thought that his society could be changed more easily from within by people like himself, and perhaps it was only chance and a world war that made your way successful. His way would eventually have been successful because of advances in communication and education.'

'Perhaps, but my way worked in my lifetime and was much more splendid and heroic.'

'Didn't he actually begin the trade union system in the island?'

'Yes, he did and I thought I would have to follow in his footsteps again. Although I was now an adult he was still bigger and stronger and I resented this. This was the first time we quarrelled because the Seamen's Union and Fishermen's Cooperation were both such sensible organisations. I decided to leave the island and learn about trade unions. That's when I travelled by schooner up and down the islands, and returned with Mr Walker, and forced Clifton out of the leadership of the Seamen's Union. That was when he joined the police force. Our knowledge and control of the Seamen's Union was useful when I needed to leave the island in a hurry.'

'What happened when you came back?'

'I found that, as a result of the agitations in all the islands, universal suffrage was becoming established in all of them and political parties were sprouting up. I still had my following but not sufficient clout to form a strong party, so I joined the strongest existing one and we have won both elections since then.'

'Have you thought of what will happen when you lose an election?'

'That is not likely to happen, but even if the party lost I would still win my seat and I am always a trade unionist.'

'I can never understand how a politician, congressman, senator can live on four-year contracts which may or may not be renewed.'

'That's probably the reason that you are not a politician.'

After Dan and John had left, their uncle continued to think of the childhood and other days.

He remembered his mother and her attempt to persuade him to go to a secondary school, and he remembered his headmaster.

George Prevost was the headmaster of the primary school attended by the Cliftons. He had no illusions about his job. He regretted the dropouts while striving for literacy. There was also a competition to provide students for secondary education. He was giving his favourite general education lesson in a geography class.

'What is an island? Land which is completely surrounded by water. Australia is a continent, not an island. Therefore size is a consideration. We are an island but we were not always so. Once upon a time we were part of a great plain connected with the Americas. It was a large fertile plain, well populated by a highly developed group of people. Then, as now, there were legends and the plain was surrounded by a fiery ring of mountains which were considered to be the end of the earth. There lived a great dragon who breathed flames that destroyed the crops if it was not worshipped properly. He had a thousand heads and a thousand mouths from which tongues of flame licked the surrounding lands. Occasionally his belly rumbled and he vomited molten rock and devoured sacrifices.

'Life was difficult unless one lived far from the ends of the earth. Distance alone did not confer safety, and the inhabitants must have sinned greatly because one day the dragon writhed in anger and roared so loudly that the plain was torn asunder, and millions of tons of water rushed in to cover the plains. When the fires were quenched and the steam dissipated, all that was left of that great plain were the mountain tops of the end of the world. For a long time these were deserted but gradually birds returned and brave explorers and outcasts from the people moved from one mountain top to the other and returned to tell tall tales of hardships, endurance and courage.'

'I don't want to go to any parade. Clifton don't have to go. Why should I?'

'Because you are still at school, Randolph, and Clifton is not,' replied his mother. 'Besides, a parade is exciting... the band playing, the guns firing and the choirs singing. You will see the police and cadets and scouts all marching ahead of you and afterwards you will have a party at the school with sweets, sweet drinks and cake.'

'I hope it rains,' said Randolph.

'So do I,' said his father. 'Everything is so dry. It ent rained at all this year yet.'

'It is Empire Day, 25 May, and all school children have to parade. It is a beautiful day, the sun is shining and it is already eight o'clock. Hurry up and get dressed, Randolph.'

Claire Lawrence had a holiday today because her infant school children were not expected to parade. Her husband and older son Clifton had come back a little earlier after a night of fishing and they had returned with a good catch which had quickly sold. So the younger son was jealous and angry at being treated like a child. Her husband Lionel was a good fisherman, owned his own boat and also the acre of land on which stood the three-roomed wooden house they all called home. He was proud of what he had achieved and so was she. However, she wished he would let this second child go on to secondary school, but there was always difficulty arguing with him. He did not know anybody who had gone further than primary school except priests and he could see no reason why anyone would want to. She wanted her children to be qualified to join the Government Service and he could see no reason why they could not be like him. She had five children and two miscarriages; two of the babies had been stillborn and one had died in infancy of gastroenteritis. Now she was left with her two boys, Clifton and Randolph, and her husband Lionel. Clifton had left school at age twelve and gone fishing with his father and Randolph wanted to go also.

Today Randolph was going to the parade. He ought to realise how good it was to be young and carefree and healthy. She got him dressed while the other two ate their breakfast and walked down to the town with him.

'Why are you coming with me today?'

'I want to go and watch the parade. Your father and your brother are tired and will be going to bed, and there is no work to do in the garden. I am coming to watch the bands and to watch you in the parade.'

'You won't see me. There are hundreds of school children marching today.'

'This is probably the last year you will be in it unless you go to college and join the cadets.'

'Not me! I want to go fishing with Pa and Clifton.'

'Wouldn't you like to wear nice suits and live in a big house?'

'I don't think so, but if I want to do that later I can always do it.'

'Not always. You need the education for that.'

'Well, Pa want me to come fishing with him.'

'You need your boy days before you start working for your living. You will be grown up soon enough.'

'I want to leave school as soon as possible.'

'All right but enjoy yourself today.'

It had been his last year at school. His family had shrunk slowly. First his father was lost at sea, and his mother died during the war while he was in the Merchant Navy. Now Clifton was dying and there was a sense of isolation and desolation. He got dressed and went off to see his brother for the last time.

★

Sarah Lawrence was returning from morning service. She was hurrying back to her vigil over Clifton but it had been good to come away and pray. The never-ending stream of visitors and sympathisers with the constant repetitive theme of speculation had been more wearying than she had realised but now, recharged, she felt guilty of desertion. Daniel and Boy recognised her as the car approached the hill. The car stopped and Daniel opened the door for her to get in. She was not used to cars and it was strange to see her son driving one, but nothing was the same again anyway. One did not spend thirty years living with another without regarding that person as part of oneself.

'Daniel, I was expecting you back this afternoon. I wanted to ask you about Pa's condition.'

'I told Lucille to tell you I would be back this evening.'

'Yes. What do you think about Pa?'

'Ma, you know there is not much hope. How was he when you left?'

'The same way. He is still not speaking.'

'I don't think he will, Ma.'

'You think that it's his agony then?'

'Yes, but he's not feeling it badly.'

'I wish he could see you and speak to you. He would like to help you I am sure.'

'You have both helped me a lot already.'

'He is a good man, Daniel. Mr and Mrs Weston think a lot about him.'

'I know, Ma.' The car stopped and they got out.

'John, go back to the hotel. I will walk up with Ma.'

They walked in silence. Daniel was embarrassed at having so little to say.

'Has Pa always been happy?'

'Why yes! He had everything he wanted. People like him. We never had any trouble.'

'Ma, if there is anything you want, now or at any time, please let me know.'

★

Janet sat brooding over her drink. The hotel was humming with life. Never before had she realised how exuberantly voluble American citizens were. The tourist boat tours of the day were over and it was the cocktail break before the night life began. The bar was doing a roaring trade and the boy was helping to wash up glasses and supply ice for the barman. She would have to move on from this place. She was becoming restless and inclined to resent the presence of other tourists. A beefy red-faced specimen was standing in front of her table.

'Hi, there! You're not from the boat are you?'

'No!'

'Guess not. I woulda recognised you. You look kinda lonely. Come over and have a drink.'

'No thanks.'

'You're an American, aren't you?'

'Yes, sort of.'

'Well, what do you mean? Sort of?'

'Well. I've lived here for a long time.'
'Gee, you're lucky! What is there to do right now?'
'What have you done today?'
'Oh! The works! The underground caves, the cliff the Caribs jumped off rather than be captured by the French, Josephine's birthplace, the hot geysers and all the quaint little villages in the forest.'
'You've certainly been around. Did you see Uncle Tom's Cabin?'
'No! Go on. You are kidding!'
'What do you mean, kidding? Tom Foster was Stephen Foster's brother and he invented the calypso and he settled down in a wonderful log cabin in the forest. Built it himself. Used to play a guitar and sing at weddings and other fêtes. His cabin is now a national monument. Pity you missed it.'
'Gee! You must know a lot about this place. Come over and join us.'
'Do you have a bet on that you can make me come over?'
'Yeah! You don't want me to lose it, do you?'
'No. But I am expecting a friend. Oh! There he is... excuse me... Peter! Peter!'
'I guess I had better be drifting back. Be seeing you.'
'Bye. Hello, Peter, have a seat. Am I glad to see you! All those tourists and this noise... and this great big bunny chaser!'
'Hello, Janet. Thought I would drop in and see how you are.'
'I'm fine. How was the great reunion with your buddy this afternoon?'
'You mean Dan? He has changed. Life's odd that way. You build up a great story about a place you've seen and enjoyed, or some friendship, and you are anxious to repeat the whole experience.'
'Yeah! And it's never the same. The cork has been left off and the fizz has gone. It's the same with old girlfriends, isn't it?'
'I wouldn't know, Janet. I haven't any old girlfriends. What are you doing tonight?'
'I hadn't planned on anything. I would hate to get mixed up with this tourist mob.'
'There ought to be lively dance here tonight.'

'Let's wait and see. Tell me about your friend.'

'Well, he's got a chip on his shoulder and is busy organising a competition of black and white.'

'What did you expect, if he was brought up here and then went to a Negro university in the States?'

'Yes, I know. Negro church, Negro seminary, I have heard it all already today.'

'Too bad. Maybe he will improve on acquaintance.'

'He must be upstairs because he has been to his parents and returned. The car I lent him is outside in the parking lot.'

'Go and find him and bring him back. It will soon be dinner-time.'

'You haven't told me what we are doing tonight.'

'Let's not make plans, Peter. There's plenty of time.'

'You haven't any regrets, have you?'

'Don't be silly, darling. I enjoyed last night very much and I do want to spend a lot more time with you.'

'I'll go and find Dan.'

Boy was busy in his small space behind the bar dealing with the never-ending stream of glasses to be washed. At his end there was the usual pocket of barflies pushed down by the traffic along the length of the bar. Conversation buzzed; punctuated by the orders for whiskies, rum collins, manhattans, mint juleps and complaints about the prices of the drinks.

'Can you beat it? A dollar-fifty for this drink?'

'Serve you right for ordering mint julep. Don't you know they have to import the julep, and the exchange of dollar for sterling is ridiculous. Then there is the import duty and the storage.'

That was Inspector Lester talking to three others. He had rescued them when their taxi had been involved in an accident. One of the party was leaning on the bar and his camera had slipped off his shoulder. His wet buck teeth flashed in a red face, bright staring eyes peered through rimless glasses and he had a bright red shirt draped over a full paunch. The camera was being pushed dangerously near the edge of the bar. It was a beautiful movie camera. The lens, uncovered, shone through the glossy leather case.

'We Americans spend a lot of money on places like this and

then they try to fleece us. They act as though the accent belongs only to millionaires.'

'Doesn't it? I thought all you Yanks came from Texas and owned oil wells.'

'Yeah! We're doing OK. We lead the world in production and distribution methods. If this sleepy old place belonged to us we could make something of it. Look at Puerto Rico.'

'Maybe,' says Red Shirt, 'but it's all inflation. The balloon is going up, but brother, when it bursts, are we going to howl.'

He leaned heavily on the bar and the camera wobbled on the edge. Boy caught it and placed it on the shelf.

'All this supporting – Vietnam, Congo, United Nations – you people in Europe did all right out of it. You got money from us. We are just handing it out. Better go and see how the little lady is doing. Hell! Where is my camera?'

'Where did you put it?'

'On this bar and I haven't moved from here.' Inspector Lester took over.

'Well, it can't have gone far. You, boy, where is the camera? Give it back at once!'

Boy stood frozen with fear.

'There it is on the shelf. Hand it back at once. Thieving little monkey! Thought you would forget it. No! Leave it where it is and call the manager.'

Meanwhile, Peter had gone up to Dan's room, where he found him unpacking.

'Hello, Dan. I have just returned from seeing your Dad. They told me you had just left. He's much worse now, isn't he?'

'Yes, I don't think he will last the night.'

'No. It looks like the end any time now. Ma finds it difficult to accept.'

'I know. She was never much interested in anyone else. She'll find life pretty grim without him.'

'Come downstairs with me and have a drink before you eat.'

'I don't fancy that crowded lounge right now, Peter.'

'We can keep away from the crowd and it won't be for long.'

'OK.'

They went down to the table where Dan was greeted by Janet.

Whiskies and soda were ordered and Janet remarked, 'Almost like Times Square, isn't it?'

'Yes, there is no escaping the effect of the mighty dollar.'

'You think tourism is essential for the island's survival?'

'Unless light industries are established it must be, and even then there will still be the problem of markets. Tourism is the easy answer. Why did you come here?'

'To get away from all this!'

There was confusion at the bar and people were turning to seek the cause. Inspector Lester was getting in to his stride.

'You'll be flogged and put in to jail, you little thief.'

'Oh, come now. No need to make a fuss. Just get my camera and call it quits.'

'That's OK for you but I have to deal with this every day of my life and if you don't stamp it out early, it just builds up. You must put the fear of God in to these people. Where the hell is the manager?'

Dan looked at Peter. Peter stood up and moved to the bar. He pushed his way to Lester.

'What is the matter, Jack?'

'That boy has stolen a camera. It belongs to that gentleman. There it is on the shelf behind the bar.'

'Here you are.'

'That's not good enough. The boy has to be punished.'

Peter looked at Boy. 'What happened?'

'It was falling off the bar and I caught it.'

'Bloody liar,' shouted Lester.

'That's enough, Jack. If you have a formal complaint to make, please do so. Otherwise, shut up.'

'This is my duty. Why are you trying to protect the boy?

'Are you making a formal charge?'

'I have been doing this for his own sake. You would prefer to see him in jail, I suppose?'

They stood glaring at each other.

'You will shut up or get out of here.'

Frank had pushed his way up to them by now and said, 'Inspector, let's go to my office.'

The inspector's glance challenged his and then he squared his shoulders and strode off. Peter glanced at Boy.

'Come on. Let's get away from here.

Janet looked at Dan. There was a hurt, defenceless look in his eye. This was much more than she could understand. 'It seemed a lot of fuss and bullying, didn't it?'

Boy lay on his bed in his room. His face was wet with tears and he was exhausted with emotion but he could see the army of red faces with black-toothed grins on the television screen. They were preparing to advance. Now was the time to use his army. He went to the armoury and checked the supply of machine guns and ammunition. Then he paused. Why should be risk the lives of his men needlessly? This was war and the biggest victory was the one involving least loss to one side. It wouldn't be butchery. He went to the central room tower, estimated the range the main force required and detonating time. The lights blinked at him as the computer worked. The adjustments were made. Once more he hesitated, switched on the television screen. There they were, the general with the pig's eyes, like the inspector, and they too had atomic warheads. His hand moved to the control button, rested a minute and then pushed.

★

Dan and Janet drove down the road between the night-scented hedges to the avenue overlooking the harbour. The bright lights shone firmly across the bay from the houses on the other side. A boat rowing across the harbour left a gleaming phosphorescent wake behind it and jewels dropped from the wings of the oars.

'What was it all about at the hotel?' asked Janet.

'It was Frank Weston's son and Peter's half-brother.' There was a pause.

'Oh, I see! That's why Peter was so angry, but how does it affect you? He was well protected.'

'He is my nephew. Do you know how it feels to stand helplessly aside when there is a disturbance like that? The feeling that one must not be involved. Tell me, if you are walking down a street and see a wallet lying on the ground, what would you do? You would pick it up, wouldn't you? Then you could examine it and all this without making up your mind what you were going to do with it. I would have to hurry past it, because if I picked it up, there would be a tap on my shoulder and it would be the owner accusing me of picking his pocket. Even if he didn't and I got as far as the police station to return it, there would be something missing and I would have stolen it.'

'You are over-sensitive. I am protected only because I can afford to defend myself. You are feeling this way because you are depressed. Tell me about your father.'

'There isn't much to tell. He would make it sound like a success story because he was content with his achievement. He was a fisherman, then a policemen, then an estate worker who became estate manager, only he never got paid as one. He never expected to be. Peter and himself were a mutual admiration society. I suppose I resented that. My father was always a competent manager. The adjoining estate belonged to the Lesters, the inspector's father. There has always been a feud between the two. We enjoyed those boyhood raids across the borders. I once got caught by Jack on his land and there was a fight. I won but it was not the end. I was thrashed by my father for that. Still, it was fun in those days and I have not regretted beating Jack Lester. Yet Pa would have been proud of Peter if he had beaten Jack Lester. I could not see why there was a difference. Then we grew up and Peter went to England, I went to Washington and Jack to training college. I knew that I would not want to come back. There were too many memories.'

A policeman came up and looked in the car.

'You better move your taxi. There is no parking here.'

'Sorry. I didn't see any 'No Parking' signs.'

'Don't give me that story. You are no stranger here. What's your name?'

'Lawrence.'

'Where is your driving licence?'

'It's American. An international licence.'

'Cho! Let me see it man.' Daniel produced his licence and the policeman glanced at it.

'Oh! You are a doctor. Are you related to Randolph Lawrence?'

'Yes, I am his nephew.'

'Glad to meet you, Doctor. You had better get a local licence. This one is not legal here.'

The policeman moved on.

'His master's voice!' said Dan bitterly. 'Trouble till he sees a licence that is not valid!'

Janet looked at him curiously.

'What are you complaining about? A moment ago you were afraid of being discriminated against and now the process is reversed you don't like it.'

'Isn't it still discrimination?'

'My dear man, all life is discrimination. People are individuals. What you are going to like, what you are going to eat, where you are going to live... the ones with the widest choice should be the happiest but that does not necessarily follow. Man is so adaptable that he can rationalise most things to appear to be a natural choice, especially when he has few alternatives.'

'We had better move from this no parking area.'

'I'm hungry! Where can we eat? You had better tell me. I have been away from this place for so long that I no longer know the place.'

'There is a Chinese Restaurant on Henry Street. Let's go there.'

★

Peter was still angry as he spoke to his father.

'I suppose you have made it up with Jack and explained that you are all big boys together.'

'There was no need for the scene you were trying to create.'

'What are you doing about Boy? Don't his feelings matter?'

'He is becoming a problem, isn't he? I wonder if I should not send him to boarding school. It would be an interesting experiment.'

Joan Weston came up to them, 'It's going to be a busy time, Frank, and on top of it you have to create more problems. You must do something about this child.'

'Yes, I was telling Peter that we could send him away to school.'

'Well, do something. Now that Clifton is dying there is nothing to keep that family together. There is quite a crowd going up that way and I suppose that we will have a noisy wake. We'd better do something about that too. What do you suggest, Peter?'

'You could get a couple of labourers to rig up a shelter with a tarpaulin against the cocoa house. A couple of charcoal stoves in oil drums would be a help. Then you could arrange for some food and drink.'

'What do you mean, 'you'? Why have I got to arrange everything?'

'Here is old man Lester coming up. I'd better get away and arrange it or I won't get a chance.'

As he moved away towards the kitchen, Paddy Lester walked up to Frank and Joan. Peter greeted him and then excused himself.

'Good evening, Frank. I hear I owe you an apology. The trouble with this country is that the girls grow up so quickly and the men remain immature. I would never have believed that son of mine would still be playing with uniforms and parades and shouting orders. It just proves that environment is more important than heredity. Aren't you going to offer me a drink? Well, I'd better be getting you one... not that I agree with you that Lent is over yet.'

Frank called a waiter and ordered drinks.

'There is no need to apologise for Jack. He considered it his duty.'

'Heaven help us! That is exactly what I am raving about. The Irish don't breed policemen. We supply you with your generals and then our writers record your triumphs and mistakes. We are the one race that has never sought to lead the western nations. Spain, France, Holland, England, Germany and Italy all tried and failed, and now America and Russia are bidding for command. You really bungled things. You preached democracy and practised aristocracy. You vaunted the value of education and ambition and denied them both.'

'What are you preaching now? More seditious nonsense?'

Lester was indignant. 'Preaching indeed! It's my son I'm grudging you and your system. I need him on the estate, not strutting up and down in uniform. I hear you are losing your manager. You won't find another like him. You have no cause to grumble though. He gave you a full lifetime and he is not even waiting for a pension. Surely no man can do more.'

'There is no future in the estate without a manager and Peter is not interested in it.'

'Times have changed haven't they, Frank? Now the hotel is more important than the estate. All those tourists about the place and you encourage them. The place won't be fit to live in soon. What kind of show are you putting on tonight?' Don't tell me! Limbo, steel band and a calypso. You ought to pay us natives for providing local colour.'

'Why is it that you and I are marooned in this ridiculous country?'

'You know quite well why we are. You were born here but I was enchanted by it on a cruising holiday. We both have done well out of it.'

'Yes, but how many others have failed? Everyone presumes it is easy to be a plantation owner but we know of dozens who have failed. You bought your estate from a failure and you have made it succeed. We know of others who have turned to drink or committed suicide because they learnt that plantation life is not easy. It is doomed anyway.'

'Why do you say that?'

'There are many reasons. The first is that the products you produce are being produced by all the third world countries and all are competing for the same markets. So the one with the cheapest labour and the cheapest product brings the price down to an uneconomic level. We only continue to find markets because there are wars, riots and disasters and revolutions in other countries. Once they have sorted themselves out we will be forced out of the market by the least developed countries.'

'What do you suggest is the answer?'

'Strange to say, the second reason why it is doomed is because of the competition for the land for building and for peasant farming. I would suggest that you look closely at the lands you possess and reserve what can be real estate for building and development and begin to sell off the rest in small parcels.'

'That is all very well but I like to work.'

'I am not saying you should not keep some and use it well. What I am saying is that the real future is in business. It is in real estate, construction, insurance, industry, banking, and in wholesale or retail outlets. That is a very wide choice.'

'Why are you giving me this lecture this evening?'

'I suppose it is because I have been thinking of it for a long time. But Clifton dying brings it to a head. I shall have to find someone to replace him, and I suppose I have to find somewhere for his wife to live. However, what I want to suggest to you is starting a bank.'

'How does one do that?'

'First we have the names of people who want to be associated with starting one and who can find the necessary capital. After that we approach government for permission and licence.'

'Why should they give you one?'

Because every country needs capital to develop and government would prefer it to be local and to ensure that local money in invested locally and does not go overseas. You and I know a dozen people to approach to set it up. Thereafter we go to shareholders. I have earmarked the site and can have the building within a year. We can finance people who want to buy lands. Or houses, or wish to start businesses, just like any other bank. As you know, I am already in the insurance and hotel business and the next obvious one to go in to would be real estate and construction.'

'You are not a young man. Why would you want to take on so much?'

'That is a very good point. Young men do not have the vision or the experience. I was hoping that Peter would be interested in all this but he chose medicine and he wanted to dabble in politics. I think he does not know where power lies and is not sure what he wants. I hope to change him and I would be glad if he got married. You have a large family so I want to bring you in to all this as well, if I can.'

'We would be happy to be a part of it. Apart from Jack, the other two boys and Fiona would like to know that there is something to come back to do. Do not give up on Peter because I am sure he can be persuaded to help. He is probably not interested in running a hotel or a store but he could be interested in what you have been talking about.'

'The fact that he was interested in politics is what gives me hope. Wealth is power and he can do a lot more for his country without going in to politics. It seems a strange thing that so few Negroes appear to desire to pursue wealth.'

'There are quite a few black businessmen!'

'Yes, but unlike Chinese and Indians, how many take their businesses beyond the stage of being comfortable? Very, very few! The pursuit of wealth for its own sake is something that requires devotion and concentration and also the quest for power.'

'Are you saying that it is a fault to be content with mere economic independence?'

'No! You, for example, are not interested in wealth and power but you wish to find good opportunities for your children. Most people behave this way and I am not being prejudiced when I say that. I am merely remarking that politics is a quest for power and for some it is the easier route, but that is not true for Peter and he will have to be convinced of this.'

'He has a problem reconciling you and the Clifton family.'

'He does not know that I put Daniel Lawrence through university and that I am prepared to look after the rest of the family after the father dies.'

'You do not have any prejudice then?'

'Prejudice is irrational and taught usually by propaganda. It is usually based on a sense of superior versus inferior and can be related to race, religion and class. It cannot be said to be related to intelligence. There we call it snobbery and the less intelligent is really inferior. You were referring essentially to racial prejudice. There were lots of attempts to prove that black is inferior in intelligence and IQ tests. Bertrand Russell himself supported that theory, and anatomists and pharmacologists and even anthropologists have tried to prove things from the shape of the skull and the bones. Most intelligent people have realised that this is not so. Intelligence can also be related to environment, class and opportunity, teaching and motivation. When you check tertiary education you find most of the races represented and all do equally well, but that the Jews and the orientals are usually the most highly motivated.'

'You still have not answered my question. You know that most of the planters agree that blacks are primitive and require two or three generations to achieve equality.'

'If you mean literacy and education then all it needs is one generation if you provide enough schools and teachers and improve the economy a little. That, however, is nothing to do with intelligence. I agree that I have no time for stupid people, but those belong to all races.'

'Why have you left out prejudice based on economics and fear and superstition?'

'Fear of competition for jobs and women underlies most prejudice. When a minority group begins to become large enough and powerful enough to upset a system, this prejudice is no longer irrational. So indeed prejudice is a defence mechanism and if we recognise it as such we would be better able to deal with it. It is a reciprocal affair between black, white, mulatto, Chinese, Christian, Muslim, Buddhist, rich, poor, strange and different. One can be prejudiced against a group and condemn the group yet be friends with individuals from that group. It is an atavistic reaction to the unknown and unknowable.'

The beach, dimmed in starlight, offered a cool evening. The sound of the waves faded in bubbles on the thirsty sand and the palm trees stirred the breeze with a slow, swaying dance. Gone was the hot haze of molten gold and the steel blue gleam of sea on which Boy's picture of Sunday picnics in violently coloured shirts had angered him. It was unchanged only because such a night always softened the edges of reality and he was once again a boy walking barefoot through a shanty town of leaning shacks and rusting galvanised roofs to the quiet of dying waves and drowsy insects.

The girl too knew this beach, not only from Sunday picnics but because of Peter and the night before and she wondered why the stage setting of these two males was so similar. Was it a symbol of perfection or lack of imagination, or had the beach a significance for these two men, Peter and Daniel?

'You came because he is dying and you wanted to see him, be acknowledged by him and blessed. You are disappointed because you can no longer be acknowledged. You have fought to have him see you as Peter's equal or better and he is still blind. Yet there is satisfaction in the fact that Peter's ministrations will be useless and that under your conditions survival would have been possible. Peter's condition and yours, both distorted and both influenced by that man who is dying, it is like a developed but unprinted roll of film, familiar but unreal.'

He looked at her shadowed face in the sand and moved his hand to touch her hair. She caught his hand.

'I want to talk to you.'

'That is all we have done tonight... talk.'

'I hope you have not been bored.'

'Since I did most of the talking, that would be odd, but I wonder why you are interested. It is because of Peter?'

'Partly, but it is also because of you. You are both strange people and I feel that you will always be strange people to me. So alike and yet you feel that you are so different.'

'The difference is that he has never had to work for success.'

'Are you not the more successful one now? Does he grudge you that success?'

'He is not interested. His little island life is enough for him. He is content. Like my father, my uncle, Peter is content with his little niche in life and therefore will resist any effort to change that pattern of life.'

'Isn't that the aim of life? Be jealous if you wish, but be honest enough to admit that it is jealousy.'

'I should have said complacency, not contentment. To be smug and self complacent can never be a virtue.'

'Like you, Peter is restless and uneasy. You both wish to carry the burdens of the world on your shoulders.'

He looked at her angrily.

'It would be an easier burden if we could have others share it and be aware of it.'

'No thanks. It is too easy to find burdens. You must learn to shed yours.'

'Temptress! On a night like this it would be easy.'

He turned and kissed her. She pushed him away but he persisted. She fought angrily.

'Stop it! Stop it!'

'Why?' he mocked.

'Because I'll scream!' She felt his hard body recoil, then relax in to limpness.

'Your Inspector Lester would be pleased, wouldn't he, especially as you are an old school pal?'

She could feel his horror of the trap. He was motionless and his face looked in to the darkness beyond her.

'You cannot prevent my accusing you, can you? That policeman saw us together and he won't forget that long chat. God, you make me sick! One touch of the whip and you cringe. You are trembling. Yet you talk of fighting. You have been well conditioned. A snarling pack of hounds controlled by one man with a whip.'

Dan felt his heart pounding and his whole body hot and soaked with sweat. His mouth was dry and open and he had been running from eternity. His was the primeval feel of the trapped animal. The first numbing shock, paralytic and analgesic when death would have been painless, then a frozen eternity of disembodiment of consciousness when one is aware of all that is happening and has ever happened, aware of the amazing clarity of perception instead of the knowledge of participation.

Now was the fighting reaction of recovery and his anger reasserted itself as terror faded in to anger at his self-betrayal and her lashing scorn. He silenced her mouth with his and she went limp in his arms.

There was no blinding flash of light, no mighty explosion, and for a moment Boy felt his plan had miscarried. Then the whole television screen was obscured as a continent heaved, shuddered and was flung to the Heavens, it seemed to contract for a moment in spasm before leaving its crater in dusty fragments. The mighty toadstool of disaster blackened the sky in many countries and there was wild speculation in all that there would be panic about fallout and the search for the enemy.

For the moment he was dismayed by his powers of destruction. Not only the general and the army but all those beautiful cities and the people who lived in them were gone. Had it been really necessary? Like Sodom and Gomorrah, the innocent had shared the penalty of the guilty. His vision of God did not allow for such wholesale destruction, greater than flood, earthquake and tidal wave. Father, he asked, did the innocent die in Sodom and Gomorrah? He knew the answer even though he could not have formed it in words. There were no innocent. The city had been warned and was aware of its sins and those who were not themselves sinners were guilty by association. Those who do not object, consent. But father, what of the babes and children? Again the answer came. They were prejudged for they too would have been guilty by association and they could not have differed from their parents under those conditions Then father, forgive me, for I am what my parents and country make me.

The monotonous chant of the litany rose and fell like waves on a deserted beach. All the saints were being invoked for aid in that little house and the '*ora pro nobis*' response beat against the walls before drifting out through the doors and windows of the building. Outside, the glow of the charcoal burners lit up the old cocoa shed and silhouetted the shapes of the men drinking coffee and rum. The hum of their conversation was audible until Lucille was some distance from the house. She felt unnecessary among the mourners and resented this. Pa did not need her even now. Unconsciously she struggled to breathe among the crowd of sympathisers. The fascination of his impending death for so many people who had little to do with his life horrified the girl. What right had they to anticipate his wake? She walked slowly down the path to the shed and took a cup of coffee from Marie. Rango, Slim and Gustave were among a group of men reliving Pa's life. All were trying to share in forgotten episodes in his life. Pa had never asked anyone for help in his life. How different these people were. They would all take as much as possible without thinking of giving anything in return.

Rango was talking.

'It go back a long time, man. Clifton and Randolph making good business fishing until Clifton start the association. He want all fisherman to get together and rent deep freeze and thing. Randolph say Clifton trying to boss everybody so Clifton stop fishing and join police.'

Slim took over.

'I remember them police days. It bad when two brothers can't pull. Randolph, he takeover head of all sort of union and Clifton he sergeant of police. Then riot breakout in the sugar factories and things go from bad to worse. Randolph leading demonstration and thing. Remember the march on Government House? Stick and cutlass in people hand and Clifton with his ten police at the gate.'

'He have no right to shoot,' says Rango. Slim looked at him.

'You there, man? I was in police and I there. Clifton say, 'Over their head the first time. If that don't stop them, you going to have to shoot for good. First round... fire! Randolph leading these big strong cutlass men... then baraaang... it was over their heads. Defeu walking next to Randolph fell down dead. There is silence den and you hear the trees shaking until Clifton voice roar like a lion, "Squad, prepare to fire!" Man, people fall down precipice and up tree and down tree and roll in bush. You never see anything like it. After that Clifton give up police and come here.'

'And Randolph go to jail,' adds Rango.

'Who worry about Randolph?' says Slim. 'He take care of himself. He even living with Clifton's daughter now.'

Lucille turned to go and saw Peter near the house, coming down the path. She hurried to meet him. She wondered how anyone could pretend to understand anyone else in this life.

★

Dan lay beside Janet on the sand. Her long, even breathing gave no indication of any emotion. His left hand made a shallow furrow in the sand as he moved it to and from.

'Janet?'
'Yes?'
'I'm sorry.'
'Are you?'
'Can I explain?'
'Can you?'
'Why did you taunt and threaten?'

She half turned on her side to look at him. For a moment she looked at his face staring at the stars.

'You are so immature. Like Frank you have been robbed. But it is not the rape of this land that makes you what you are. One could forgive the thief and despoiler. You cringe at the whip, you withdraw from the real battles. Every conqueror propagates his own psychological brainwashing to condition himself to rule and his subjects to remain servile. That's the pity. You and your generation will never be rid of the brand or the yoke across your shoulders.

'The danger is even greater because as you assume more responsibility, the only alternative is to become the master. Not as he is in his homeland, but the conditioned master you know and hate, and you in your turn will demand more slaves. That is the tragedy of your inheritance and the unforgivable legacy of your masters.'

'Janet, this land I hate and love. On a night like this she gives so much, and her dawns are cool whispers of promises. Her restless fevered days can be a delirium of emotion cured only by the bewitchment of another night. When I am away I can dream of her beauty and be content for her to fill the evening of my days. To be back here is like returning to the spell of a mistress of impossible promises... hopeful and futureless. I can see why others are content with the tastes of delight, whetting the appetite and promising fulfilment. I know it is a delusion because as you say, there is too much past to face in the lonely hours, a past when her favours were not mine, a future of striving for a greater share of those favours at the expense of others. That is why I feel I must not stay here.'

There, where Peter sat, the table on the crowded dance floor, was surrounded by his father, Lester, and son. The steel band's jangle and the cool clink of ice on the sweated glass, the burning taste of whiskey on the rocks... none of these had made the waiting for Janet's return any easier, the taste of her mouth was still on his and the feel of her body demanded the ritual of renewal. His father's mocking glance read all this with pitiless ease.

'Where is Jan? His best friend, yes,' Frank explained to Lester. 'He'll fly in today, just so, and take her away.'

'It's always the same. These tourists always prefer the real local talent.'

Peter glared at the young Lester, 'Can't you keep your bloody mouth shut?'

'Now then,' Paddy Lester intervened quickly, 'no fights over a lady. There are too many other things to fight about.'

Peter's chair grated backwards as he stood up.

'Don't be silly,' said his father. 'Where do you think you are going?'

'I had better see about the shed at the Lawrence's.'

'Oh, very well, but come back and enjoy yourself. They'll be back soon.'

He walked in to the night. The familiar path seemed a nightmare walk. How quickly had his world changed in two days.

'Singing, I was at peace, above the clouds, outside the ring. Yet living here, as one between two massing powers I live, whom neutrality cannot save, nor occupation cheer.'

He moved past the little house with its oasis of light and its chant of litanies, to the loud clatter of the shed and, looking up, he saw Lucille hurrying towards him. He felt the protective concern he knew was his reaction to Lucille troubles.

'What is the matter, Lucille?'

'Nothing, nothing, Peter. I was glad to see you because there was so much chat of nonsense in there.'

'What nonsense?'

'Only Rango making cracks about my being with Uncle Randolph.'

'Why is he making cracks at you?'

'Oh, it's the same old talk about Pa's young days, and one thing led to another.'

'Why doesn't Rango respect the place on a night like this?'

'Well, he was the foreman of the gang working on the roads, the one I worked in. He expects women to be his when he wants them. He even offered to marry me when his passes were getting him nowhere. That's why I left the gang.'

'You should not have gone there in the first place, Lucille. Anyway, let's go back. I want to see the work for myself.'

They walked past the oil drums, chatting to each group as they passed and treating Rango's group as indifferently as the others. They had a cup of coffee at the last one. They met Randolph as they walked back. He looked away from Peter to Lucille.

'Don't worry about the expenses, child. Let me have all the bills afterwards and if there is anything you need now let me know.'

'It's already been taken care of, Mr Lawrence.'

'We don't need any conscience money, doctor. I would prefer to settle it all myself if you don't mind.'

Lucille intervened.

'Please don't start arguing now. You two will never understand each other and this is no time for trying.'

Randolph turned and walked back with them to the house.

Rango looked after them.

'A man don't have a chance there. It have too much competition.

★

The first big drops of rain fell, splattering on the dry earth, and clouds piled up over the face of the moon. Everyone scampered for shelter.

Lightning shivered the black steel of the sky and the shattered sound was echoed in the rumble and crash of the thunder. The windscreen wipers waved furiously to clear the path of glass and Janet snuggled closer to Dan.

'Exciting, isn't it? I have always felt like this about thunderstorms since I was a child. I love the sound of the rain drumming on a tin roof, the electric atmosphere and the recurring climax of thunder and lightning.'

'You need not try to reassure me. I feel it too. A sense of grand isolation, making you the God who has arranged it all.'

The road was a shining black floor in the headlamps and on it danced thousands of invisible feet, splashing to the quick beat of the music. The trees thrashed wildly in rooted despair and the wind howled with the frenzy of desire.

'It's a bit early for this kind of weather. Not exactly what we like to show the tourists.'

'Really? I suppose it is your black secret soul of torment and not your bright shining smile.'

He looked at her out of the corner of his eye. He saw a light around the bend. The next moment the high blinding light of a truck pinned him to the road and the thunder of the crash flung him against her. His arms were around her as he heard the scream of the brakes, then the excited chatter of the men jumping from the truck. He leaned past her and opened the door, then slid by to examine her more closely. The red-gold mask of hair hid her face and as he brushed it back he felt the wet bruise on her temple. Her limp form stiffened and her lips moved to moan. His relief set his heart beating and the blood roaring in his ears. He had not yet seen the crowd of men around him or heard their questions. Now he turned to them.

'Phone for an ambulance. I'll stay here with her.'

To hide his shaking knees he had to sit on the floor of the car and hold her hand.

★

Peter, Randolph and Lucille struggled past the group in the front room. Sarah, sitting beside the bed, looked up at them.

'He's sleeping now. The rain woke him and he asked for Lucille. Do you think he is going to get better?'

Peter looked at the form breathing deeply and smoothly on the bed and the doctor's curiosity drove him instinctively to reach for the wrist. Clifton opened his eyes and looked slowly from one face to another.

'The rain... it drives such strange ones together... from all the holes and cracks and under the stones.'

'Dan is coming to see you.'

'No, Dan's life is always in tomorrows. He is too busy for ordinary todays. I want to talk to you, Peter, alone.'

The others looked at each other and moved out to the front.

'I was not fair to Lucille, Peter. You wanted advice and I gave you what I thought you wanted to hear. I strengthened your doubts but I hoped you would do otherwise. Look after her for me, Peter.'

'Don't let it worry you. Try to get some rest.'

'That is good advice. I like to sleep with the sound of rain, and death is not a fête for the dying.'

'I wish I could do more for you, Clifton.'

'It's enough, Peter. Keep them away from me. It's good to know you are all there, but not to pity. Grieve because I will not be there to help.'

He closed his eyes and Peter sat down beside him for the vigil he had promised. The rain drummed on the roof with hypnotic monotony. The buzz of whispers from the front room anticipated the song of the frogs which would follow the rain. Dan would be here soon. He wondered where he was. He could trust Janet to comfort him. It was so easy to comfort if one did not accept the obligation to remain the comforter of one fool. That was the role of husbands and wives. Only doctors and social workers could afford the other. Lucille's hand on his shoulder woke him from his doze. Her lips close to his ear brushed his cheek as he turned his head to see her.

'Peter, a message from the hospital – they want you to go there. Dan has been in an accident and someone is badly hurt.'

He looked at Clifton sleeping peacefully and nodded.

'Sit here, Lucille, and don't let anyone disturb him.'

Conflict

The rain drummed on the tarpaulin roof, which sagged in the middle under the weight of the pool of water. The fires had gone out and the sheltering crowd huddled together looking out over the sea of mud where footsteps had broken the grass. Rango had been forced to shelter there and could not escape the taunts of his companions.

'You think Lucille go work on the road now she fader die?'

'No, man, she going to marry Rango.'

'But if she work on the road she don't have to marry him.'

'That's if she work with Rango. He not going to have no 'come now, pay later' scheme no more. He learn his lesson already.'

'You think he really want she that bad?'

'Man, you fisherman and you ask that! It's always the biggest bestest one that get away and you always look for that.'

'Poor Rango! Shame he can't change his skin.'

'It ain't skin only, man. It class too. If he became engineer or buy land he have it made.'

'You think so? No man. Lucille bleach his skin for him first.'

'It's a good thing he don't have a chance then. White nigger worst thing on earth.'

The appreciative audience tittered and Rango stirred angrily.

'You boys hell, eh! The man dying and you talking about his daughter like a whore.'

'No Rango, she going to be a lady no matter what happen, she wonder if you making the grade.'

'Niggers always jealous of their superiors.'

'And nigger boss always the most superior.'

'All right, white boss always the best boss, always will be, you bloody, black bastards.'

'You not a bastard too, Rango? Tell me who your mother marry.'

The crowd was edging away from Gaston and Rango, waiting for the inevitable fight. They stood, dim forms facing each other in the dark but the hurt angry eyes were hidden.

'Alleluia! Happy Easter! The rain stop!' shouted the peacemaker and the crowd dribbled out in to the mud.

The dance was in full swing at the hotel in the early hours of the morning. Enough drink had been imbibed by all who were still there to focus all the happiness of the world on this one place. They were all friends together and even the extravagant behaviour of some could be ascribed to natural exuberance or tolerated as a weakness in human nature of one who could not hold his liquor as well as the others. The music was loud but the members of the band were enjoying themselves after their drink break. Conversations were unnaturally loud and unrestrained but no one was interested in listening to the talk of other groups outside his own. The world was relaxed and mellow and what was happening outside this world was of no interest to anyone in it.

Inspector Lester was still there, entertaining his group with anecdotes of the stupidity of criminals. In a small community like this they were marked men and could always be rounded up and interrogated to account for every crime. In fact, they would be made to do detective work to incriminate their brethren rather than be held responsible themselves. They could not emigrate after having established a police record and in effect became police auxiliaries. It was interesting and entertaining to reflect that one could expect more help from those than from the so-called law-abiding citizens.

A waiter came up to him and told him Sergeant Thomas was waiting outside to speak to him. He looked up and for a moment was annoyed at having his monologue interrupted. Then he decided that perhaps he could prove his point to his friends.

'Malfini, eh? Well, show the sergeant in, man. Ask him to come and see me here.'

The waiter walked away and Lester explained to his friends

that the nickname 'malfini' meant 'chicken hawk', and was the community's name for the sergeant. There was no time to elaborate because the sergeant was crossing the floor. There was an exaggerated salute and the loud 'sir'.

Sergeant Thomas was not going to let his boss down, especially when he had drink in him and was in the circle of his friends.

'Well, Sergeant, what is it this time?'

'I wish to report an accident, sir.'

'Really, Sergeant, at this time of night it is hardly necessary to disturb me for this. Can't you handle it yourself or must I do everything?'

'The parties involved, sir, were a banana truck and a hired car driven by an unlicensed driver.'

The sergeant's speech was becoming more staccato and parade ground material as he strove to avoid further criticism.

'Well, have you booked the driver?'

'The driver was Dr Daniel Lawrence, sir, and his companion was Miss Janet Martin. The lady has been seriously injured and has been taken to hospital.'

'What are the nature of her injuries?'

'Head injuries, sir. She has a fractured skull and is unconscious, and the doctor reports that she may not recover consciousness.'

'Which doctor are you referring to?'

'Dr Chalmers, sir. I have his report and also a statement from Dr Lawrence.'

'And where is Dr Lawrence now?'

'At the hospital, sir.'

'Very well, Sergeant. Let me have the reports and wait outside for me and I will interrogate Dr Lawrence myself.'

The sergeant was pleased. There was the step back, the stamp of feet, the stiff shivering salute, the 'sahh' in a loud voice before his turn and marching exit.

The inspector looked around for Frank Weston, then stood up and excused himself. Frank was sitting with Lester's father over in a corner and they were looking across at him. He walked over and faced Frank.

'There has been an accident, Frank, and one of your guests has been seriously injured: Janet. I am going over to the hospital now. Daniel Lawrence is in big trouble now. Driving without a licence, probably drunk, and maybe manslaughter.'

Old man Lester looked at his son.

'So you are going to help cheer him up!'

'I have my duty to do, Dad.'

'Yes, yes, a painful duty. God help you, boy!' The Inspector flushed and turned away abruptly.

The sergeant was waiting by the jeep outside and they climbed in and drove off to the hospital. He was shown in to Dr Chalmer's office and he verified the facts and the statement.

'Can't she have an operation?'

'There is no one here competent to do this.'

'May I speak to Dr Lawrence?'

'Certainly. I will call him for you. By the way he is very upset, so don't keep him too long.'

'Very well.' Daniel came in and looked at Lester and the sergeant.

'Well, Lawrence, you have done it again. No licence, careless driving under the influence of drink, and ending in manslaughter.'

Daniel was tense and sweating but his voice was well controlled.

'You have my statement, Lester, and I have nothing to add at the moment.'

'Do you realise that this case has to be investigated and there are some serious aspects? You should be arrested pending the statement from the girl. I understand that she is most unlikely to make one. She is an American citizen and it may have international consequences.'

'I wish to remind you that I, too, am an American citizen. If you will excuse me I have work to do.'

★

Peter stopped the car outside the hospital and walked in. The ambulance was still there unattended and the whole hospital was lit up. There was not the usual atmosphere of dying and convalescing. He walked in to the ward and asked the nurse for Dr Lawrence.

'He is with Dr Chalmers in the private ward.'

'Will you call him for me please?'

'Certainly, Doctor.'

The nurse was only too pleased to leave the ward and go to the focus of excitement. She hurried away and soon Daniel was back with her, looking worried and harassed.

'I had to send for you, Peter. We have been in an accident and Janet is unconscious. I thought she was not badly hurt when she began to regain consciousness, but she is now completely comatose. She has been X-rayed and there is a fractured skull. It must be an extradural haemorrhage but Chalmers won't operate. Something must be done, Peter.'

'Let me look at her, Dan, and then I will speak to Chalmers.'

Peter could feel his antipathy to Dan disappearing as he realised his concern. He walked to the only private room the hospital possessed, glanced at Chalmers and then at Janet. The pale still form was not reassuring. He felt her pulse, looked at her eyes and then at the chart. Chalmers had come up beside him.

'Lawrence is right. The X-rays, the focal signs, the history all point to a right extradural. There is nothing we can do here.'

'Haven't you got any trephines or burrs?'

'Yes, but we have never used them.'

'You had better get them ready because you will have to use them tonight.'

'Do you realise what you are saying? This is a tourist, and an American, not someone local. If she dies while we are operating there will be an inquest, a court case and a suing for damages.'

'This is a human being, and the only chance she has is an immediate operation. Get the instruments ready.'

'I'm sorry. I will not operate.'

'Then I will have to. Prepare the theatre and have her head shaved at once.'

Relieved, Chalmers hurried off to attend to the theatre. Daniel was becoming more agitated.

'Have you ever done one of these, Peter?'

'No. Have you? Would you like to do it yourself?'

'No, no. I'm a physician.'

'Well, here one must be prepared to do anything. We cannot afford specialists. Will you assist me?'

'Of course I will.'

The nurse came in armed with scissors and razor, soap and a bowl of water.

'Shave the whole head will you?'

'Yes, Doctor.'

The two doctors left the room and went over to the theatre. Chalmers came out.

'They will be ready in twenty minutes. You won't need an anaesthetist, will you?'

'No, I'll use a local, if any anaesthetic becomes necessary. I'd better get changed and check the instruments. Who is in theatre tonight?'

'The duty nurse is attending to the sterilising but she has called the theatre sister. She will be here soon.'

They went in to the room adjoining the theatre and changed in to white shirts and trousers. There was little inclination for conversation as the ritual of preparation began. Dan was even more concerned when he saw the operating theatre and checked the comparison with the ones he was accustomed to seeing.

'If it is going to be too much of a strain on you, Dan, you can wait outside.'

'No thanks, Peter, I'll manage.'

They scrubbed and washed silently, side by side, and then Peter moved off to don his gloves and gown. Having done this there was nothing to do but wait, and waiting was the greatest strain. Fortunately, the instrument trolley came clattering in from the sterilizing room and Peter moved over to examine the instruments. The theatre sister came in cheerfully and took charge of proceedings. She greeted them all, issued a series of instructions, checked the instruments, demanded more nurses and sent for the patient. Peter felt his armpits wet with sweat and knew that under his gloves his hands too would be slippery with moisture. Dan moved over to see the shining instruments. When the operation began he would become absorbed and steady, but it was always the beginning that seemed shaky.

'The burrs are new.'

'Yes, they have probably never been used. Some enthusiastic doctor must have ordered them once.'

Janet was wheeled in and transferred to the operating table. The bandages were removed from her head, exposing a naked round scalp. Cleansing and draping were a silent torture.

'Dan, you will have to apply some pressure on one side of my incision to control bleeding.'

Dan nodded. The first quick stroke was a hurried desecration and there after it was a business of controlling the haemorrhage and moving on to the end of another job.

★

Lucille watched her father dying. She knew that he was conscious but did not wish to talk, and she wondered what he was thinking. Was there anything he would have wanted to do differently? She wondered, but she felt she knew that in his self-sufficient stubbornness he would deny it. She and Dan and Pa were like that. Yet even in her short life there were many things she would have liked to change.

Boy... Boy she hoped would now be a comfort to her. She would go away with Dan and Boy and start a new life. One had to emigrate or conform. She did not wish to conform and her whole life had been a rebellion, an attempt to crash the inner circle. It was difficult enough for a man but for a woman it was obviously impossible. Marriage had seemed the only answer, but Peter was so indecisive and vacillating.

Pa loved him. Why did love blind one so completely? She loved Peter too, but a Peter she could help and change. Now it was all over. She should have realised it a long time ago and left. In her lifetime it could not be changed, but she could have helped it along in her own way just as Uncle Randolph and Pa. Poor Pa, I really thought he had helped. Perhaps that was why he did not care to talk. It would be awful to have one's illusions shattered when there was no more to undo. No more time!

She had wasted so much herself and so many other people

were wasting theirs. The worst were the conformers. The apes like Rango who helped to build up and support the illusion. Yet there is a time for arguments and this was no time for arguing with Pa. Every life must have a time when things are settled and decided... a pause... a change of life... yet no change. One reviewed it all and decided that the best was past and it had not been so bad after all. The way had been chosen and there was no turning back. One just followed it to the bitter end and made it seem a reasonable decision. It was like placing your life earnings on a horse and explaining why it should have won.

She found herself nodding and there was a silence she could not understand. Was she dreaming or was it the time of the angel's visitation? It did not matter. Nothing mattered.

She moaned and moved, there was no need for hurt. The car was moving out of control. The policeman had said something. Something about a taxi and a licence. She opened her eyes and the light forced them to close again. She turned her head away and opened them again slowly. The room was strange and so were the two men staring at her. She felt weak, and the desire to laugh hurt her head. It would be so strange to ask them where she was and why. Her hand strayed up to the bandage on her head.

'Jan, Jan, everything is all right now. I'll call the nurse to sit with you.'

Which one had spoken she could not say. They looked like negative and positive prints of the same picture – perhaps they were one.

'Dan, I'll go and call the nurse.'

Her hand was being fondled and she was not sure whether to withdraw it or not, but the concern on the face reassured her. The nurse crept in, uncertain of her role, and turned to go out again.

'I'll have to phone the police, they want a statement as soon as she wakes.' She walked out.

'Peter, she is in no fit state to make statements. You will have to tell them, since I am involved. Lester wants to press the charge of driving without a licence but I have already admitted it. That makes a statement unnecessary.'

'He probably wants her to say how fast and dangerously you were driving. Dan, don't worry. He won't have a statement tonight.'

Moonlight on a beach... yes... which one of them reminded

her of such a wonderful experience? Or was it both? Her head hurt her so much. It must be important to remember, but scenes and emotions reminded her of men. Perhaps it should be the other way round. Too late for that now, because this was a hospital and there must have been an accident. Dan and Peter these were, but there had been a Paul, too, and others. It was too difficult to relive one's life in a few moments. She must ask questions.

'What have you done to my hair?'

'We had to shave it off for the operation.'

'Operation? Why?'

'You were in an accident. A truck ran in to a car and you were unconscious.'

'When did this happen?'

'Last night when I took you out.'

'Did we go to the beach?'

'Yes.'

'It was lovely. Thank you for taking me. I had better sleep now. So tired and my head hurts.'

'Nurse will give you an injection for the pain.'

'Don't leave me... the policemen...'

'Don't worry. We won't leave you.'

Inspector Lester bustled in and looked from one to the other.

'How is she?'

'She is recovering but she is still disoriented. She can remember nothing of the accident.'

'I want a statement. Can I ask her a few questions?'

'Not now. Perhaps tomorrow she may remember a little more and perhaps it will take a few days. Amnesia is very variable.'

Janet opened her eyes again.

'Does he want a dying declaration?'

'You are not dying, Janet.'

'We are all dying... each day we die... our yesterdays are all dead. Only the ghosts insist on returning. *Toujours les revenant!* Peter and Paul and Daniel in the lion's den.'

'Try and get some sleep. Nurse, give her the injection. Lester, come with me. We can talk outside.'

Outside the hospital, Daniel explained how the accident had

happened, and Peter told him that he had no cause for concern. He pointed out that an American licence was valid for at least a week after arrival so that no charge was possible. If it were not so he would not have lent him the car.

'I am sorry I have wrecked your car.'

'I am happy that it has not turned out more seriously than that.'

'I seem to be in your debt so heavily now. Jack would have loved a charge of manslaughter due to dangerous driving. I suppose I have to retract the statement about how useless doctors are in underdeveloped countries, since you have obviously saved Janet's life.'

'That does not happen too often, so you were mostly right anyway. I now have to decide whether to join my father in his business or go away to finish surgical studies.'

'It seems a shame to waste all those years of study, but that is a decision you will have to make for yourself.'

Peter was exhausted. There had been too much to do tonight but he must pass back and see Pa before going to bed. He had left Dan to look after Janet. The house was quiet after the rain and there was only a light in Pa's room. Why did he suddenly think of him as Pa and not as Clifton? He must be tired. He went past the sleeping forms in the front room and looked in. Lucille was fast asleep, holding her father's hand. Her breathing was even and quiet and there was no other sound in the room. He picked her up and carried her out, past the sleepers and out in the open. Dawn was returning the colours to the sky and the trees. He paused, uncertain of what to do next. *This is crazy,* he thought. *What am I doing and why?* Lucille stirred in his arms and opened her eyes.

'Peter?'

'Yes, Lucille?'

'I must be dreaming.' She put her arms round him and he sat on the stone step.

'Lucille, wake up! Dan says you are going away with him.'

She opened her eyes again and looked at him. The softness firmed in to hard reality.

'Yes, I was only dreaming. I thought we were married.'

She sat up and moved to sit beside him, and smoothed out her dress .

'Life is strange. Isn't it, Peter?'

'Lucille, I know it is a strange time to ask you this. Will you marry me?'

'Why, Peter? Because of Boy, or Pa, or of Dan? Or maybe because of Janet?'

'Because of you, Lucille. I love you and you belong to this place. Will you?'

'Are you sure you won't change your mind again?'

'Yes, I am sure now.'

'Go home, Peter, get some rest. If you still want to marry me the answer will always be 'yes'. I'll walk with you to the car.'

'We'll change Boy's name to Weston and adopt him. It's his right, isn't it?'

'Yes, Peter.'

★

Easter Sunday's bright, washed face was mirrored in the eager smiling faces streaming from the church, and the hills held the echoes of the bells celebrating the end of the Mass. The little groups of people lingered outside the church and discussed the arrangements for the funeral. The sermon had been on the unexpectedness of death and the need for a constant state of preparation. Yet a funeral always seemed a reprieve and not a warning. Death had chosen other sacrifices and would be sated for a while. Now the circumstances could be discussed, and it was a relief to sympathise with the bereavement of others. It would not be a big funeral because Dan was arranging it and not the Westons. It was odd that Dan's wishes were so readily accepted by the others. Yet there would be a big following because everyone wanted a share in the last act of someone else's play. After the preliminary discussions, the groups splintered and moved off to the seclusion of their homes and their friend's houses to continue the speculations about the reactions of the two families concerned.

In a small community there is no need for funeral invitations to participate in the drama of death. Everyone was a playwright and contributed his line to the story. One listened, one borrowed, one embroidered and then passed it on. Flowers were gathered with the titbits of information and woven in to the designs of the wreaths. The men spiced their drinks with speculations of how drunk Dan had been the night before and whether the police would press charges of drunken driving. How valid was a dying declaration?

They waited in the bright sun for the bells to toll. The back room was shuttered and black, and the front room too small to hold more than the coffin and the wife and daughter of the dead. Boy was fascinated by the brown gleaming box, and polished cedar wood with its grained intricate pattern and the quick silver glint of its metal ornaments. There was the tenseness of waiting in all the strained faces; waiting for time to catch up to this moment and start a train of movement. They were like actors waiting for their cue. Inside were the two weeping women, outside the stiff black figures of the pall-bearers and a little distance away the small group of labourers.

Paddy Lester seemed the most ill at ease. He was wondering why he had been chosen and why he had accepted the post of pall-bearer. It was for Peter's sake mostly, but also for Frank, and his son, Jack.

He had never been a close friend of Clifton. It was many years now since he had had any long talk with him. As a young man when he had first come out to manage the estates he now owned, he had sought advice from Frank and been referred to Clifton. It had been easy to be friends then, to offer to employ him with more pay and better conditions. Even now, years after living on this island, he could not understand this loyalty to a master which was so much taken for granted by servant and master alike. Then came the intervening years while Jack grew up, sought Peter's friendship while rejecting Daniel's, the constant feud, the steadily mounting animosity he had mistaken for a childish pattern of behaviour, yet it had kept him away from Clifton when he could have helped by maintaining a show of friendship. How much could one blame oneself for the mistakes, the unstudied indifference that wove a pattern of misunderstanding and misinterpretation? How much was dictated by social custom on both sides, a blind acceptance of an existing state, unlikely to be changed by the eccentric behaviour of the individual? There was poor Peter for instance, distrusted by both sides, and achieving nothing. Perhaps Clifton's death would free him from his sense of guilt.

Randolph was also uneasy, there was so much Clifton and he could have done together until the day he looked down the barrel of a rifle at his brother's eyes. Not that he would not have done the same thing if conditions had been reversed. His reasons would have been different. Clifton had been doing his duty as effectively as he could and not seeking advancement. He had lacked the gift of vision and therefore the planning beyond the day's needs. He would have been surprised by death but not daunted. It had simply been the last day's work and the last night's sleep. Daniel was more like him and less like his father, but he spent too much time fighting himself. Peter was the sentimental, impractical man Clifton had made him.

The bell throbbed one long deep note and everyone moved towards the coffin. The pall-bearers lifted it out to the labourers who shouldered it and began to pad their way down the stone path, their bare feet were steadier on the uneven surface than the pall-bearers would have been. Daniel walked beside his mother and did not attempt any conversation. He knew how empty her life was, how difficult it would now be to remain a shadow of what did not exist.

The sun filtered the strange shadows of the procession through the trees lining the path and erased them with light as they moved on. Peter walked with Lucille and Boy, and saw the path, the house, the trees as Clifton's work and wondered how effective a monument this would be of one man's toil. He knew the answer.

The path would become a drive, the house a larger mansion in which Lucille and himself or some other couple would live.

He could have done more for Clifton. He should have lent him money to buy land and establish himself on his own estate. It had never occurred to him, or apparently to Clifton. Life had seemed secure and comfortable, and timeless, until now.

The path flowed in to a road where the large black hearse stood waiting, and the chatter of the mourners was hushed at the sight of the small procession. Frank and Joan Weston were waiting in the hotel car standing behind the hearse. The other mourners would have to walk.

Down by the church, the usual crowd awaited the funeral cortège. The church bell tolled dolefully every minute. A group in the crowd was discussing the death.

It was very strange. No one knew what had caused him to fall. A blackout? Dizziness? A stroke? All were most unlikely in a healthy man and Clifton had always been a healthy man. It must have been obeah: a spell on him by one of his enemies.

These were the people he had chased off the estate or arrested and charged with larceny. Besides, they hinted he had other enemies from long ago who wanted revenge. That was much more likely to be the cause of a bizarre accident.

Another group speculated on the probable theme of the priest's sermon at the funeral. Surely it would be about the one talent which was returned unused, buried and wasted. Although they had known and liked Clifton, they had to admit that he could have been a more dominant figure in the community, like his brother, for instance.

The hearse drove in to view, followed by two cars containing Lester and Peter and the Westons, and a taxi with the Lawrences. The hearse stopped at the church entrance and the pall-bearers turned out to be Randolph and Daniel Lawrence and Sarah Lawrence's brother; Paddy Lester, Peter Weston and Frank Weston made up the rest. The gleaming cedar coffin with silver handles was carried in and met by the priest at the church entrance. There were a few prayers and the pall-bearers wheeled the coffin to the altar rail. The crowd infiltrated to fill the pews. The priest read the gospel about the resurrection and said a few words, before calling on Randolph Lawrence to read the eulogy. There was a wave of whispering which ceased as Randolph began to speak.

'He was my brother. As such I consider myself most competent to provide a full assessment of the man, the boy, the child.

'We grew up together in that earlier world with parents, relatives and teachers in our own special community. As an elder brother he had special responsibilities, which he acknowledged, and so gained the respect and admiration of his younger brother and others in that small community. He never considered himself an original thinker or innovator but he was one who served. Despite that, as a very young man he founded the first working union at much the same time as these were beginning in the other Caribbean territories and so he showed an awareness of the wants and needs of his community at that time. He was always thus. He had his feet always firmly planted on this earth and he had no desire to transcend earthly things. He was for order versus chaos and law versus anarchy. As a policeman that was his role and he performed it admirably, rising to the highest position possible for his kind at the time.

'When he left that service, he returned to the role of provider. He managed the largest estate in this island and returned to his first love; as a boy he could make the soil produce and his animals flourish. This was merely on a larger scale and his sense of order soon made it in to the most successful. Even here, he kept his ear to the ground and was aware of all that occurred in the territory so that he became an advisor to a wide range of people in this community.

'You would say that I would not know of his thoughts and actions at this stage of his life and you would be wrong. We did communicate. We did see each other. Although our paths had diverged, I still sought and valued his advice, even though we each reserved the right to criticise each other. He was not restless but was always active. His abilities were manual rather than cerebral. He could repair an engine, strip and assemble a gun, yet plant the most delicate seedling.

'A community is blessed if it has a sufficient number of such practical people and so by example and encouragement he tried to teach and produce these people for the community. We grieve his loss because he cannot be replaced and because we feel we have lost him too soon. There would have been a time and a place for this later, since the end is always inevitable, and perhaps we are being selfish because we realise how few of us will have touched so many of our community and have left so much to remember.

'He goes back to the earth he has loved, in the land he has served and loved, and if there are rewards we can be certain that he has merited his share.

'He was the salt of the earth.'

Following the ceremony the pall-bearers moved the coffin down the aisles and in to the hearse. They then all followed the hearse, walking at a steady pace the long mile along the asphalt road with its regular drains and concrete borders, down to the cemetery. There, many hymns were sung while the body of Clifton Lawrence was lowered in to the grave. The Lawrence family and Peter Weston stood together and tears rolled down the cheeks of young John Lawrence. It was his first funeral. The others had all been there before and among the elders there was always a sigh of relief that their time had not yet come. They surreptitiously eyed each other, wondering whose would be the next funeral.

The grave was filled and most of the mourners returned to Sarah Lawrence's house to share her grief for the rest of the day and through the night.

★

Boy floated on his back and watched the sunset.

He leadeth me beside the still waters. Wash, oh wash away my tears, oh Lord. Why did I cry and show the world my grief? Uncle Peter had not cried. Hold my hand, what was the poem he had quoted?

'...Move then with new desire
For where we have built and love
Is no man's land.'

The shore is far away but I am a neglected sacrifice and cannot be harmed. You did not want my life for Pa's but you accepted the son of Abraham.

The police launch circled the beach of tourists and Inspector Lester was explaining to Red Shirt his detestation of powerboats and waterskiers menacing the shores. The throttle was opened and the launch leaped forward. There was no way of avoiding Boy. Only the thud was heard. A fish pot? But fish pots do not bleed and the ever-widening stain of red was blood.

Circle once again, pick up the burden and hurry back to hospital while yet the mangled body breathes. Mark well the spot, how far from shore, how unexpected.

The inspector was ill at ease in this room. He felt the disadvantage of being on unfamiliar ground and in the enemies' territory and he wondered why he had not insisted on an interview in his office instead. Yet ministers have to be humoured and the old scoundrel had said that it was important and urgent. He knew that Randolph Lawrence had little respect for the police, having suffered at their hands in the past. The man had a police record and yet now was virtually head of the ruling party. That was the result of giving illiterate people the right to vote. He wished the man would hurry up and get it over, so that he could get back to work.

Randolph walked in.

'Good evening, Inspector. I'm sorry I have kept you waiting. Please sit. Can I get you a drink?'

'No thanks.' The idea was tempting but it would only prolong the affair.

'Are you sure? I would like to have one myself. It has been a very busy and trying week for me. There have been too many tragedies in the family and as a result there is still much to do this evening. I was getting dressed to go out when you arrived.'

'But I thought you said you wanted to see me tonight.'

'Oh yes! It is important to have your official opinion on one or two matters. Legal technicalities always confuse me. I would like some expert advice.'

'Well, if I can be of any assistance, please let me know.'

'There is the question of the boy, John Lawrence. He was killed, as you know. Will there be an inquest?'

'Yes, in all cases of accidental death there must be an inquest.'

'Will this inquest be before or after his funeral? I mean, do we have to delay the burial until after the inquest?'

'No, it takes some time to arrange an inquest.'
'I see. That may take weeks or months, I suppose.'
'It may. That will be for the coroner to decide.'
'I suppose that technically it was manslaughter, wasn't it?'
'It was an accident.'
'I have heard all the details. You know this accident is unfortunate and death is always distressing. There should be some law about power boats and their approach to beaches, don't you think?'
'Yes... but in this case—'
'I know there are always exceptions. The boy was my nephew, but that fact does not influence me very much. He was never someone I would be proud of – an illegitimate child of a girl of sixteen, begotten by her employer. Indeed, he was living example of an attitude I detest. I hate to see my people considered as playthings and possessions. I feel that they still need protecting and it is my duty to see that they are protected. I hope I will have the support of the police force?'
'We will always do our duty, but I don't see how—'
'No, of course not. It is purely a social problem. Yet was the police launch on official patrol that morning?'
'It was.'
'Do you normally carry passengers or guests on patrol?'
'No. This was a courtesy extended to a visitor.'
'The drinks were also purely for the guests, I suppose?'
'Now, look here—'
'No need to get excited, Inspector. I am looking but I see an inquest coming up as well. Suppose we change the subject. I have another nephew, Daniel Lawrence. I understand there is a charge against him as well. Could you tell me exactly what the charge is?'
'Well, the case is being investigated, and since the lady claims that she was driving and she possesses a licence, it is unlikely that any charge will be brought against your nephew.'
'He is anxious to return to the States. I presume there would be no objection?'
'Not at the moment, but if the lady were to die, it would be a more serious matter.'
'I thought you said that she had stated that she was driving. Would her dying alter that?'

'No, but—'

'I suppose you have a record of her statement.'

'She has not been well enough to sign one.'

'I suggest, Inspector, that it is important that you obtain that statement and record. Life is so uncertain.'

'I will attend to it tonight.'

'Very well, Inspector, now will you have a drink?'

'No, thanks. I still have some work to do tonight and I have to leave now, if you don't mind.'

'Thank you for coming, Inspector. Goodnight.'

A child's death is always more distressing than an adult's. There are so many promises left unfulfilled. When one death follows so closely on another in the same family it becomes a lot more tragic, and Lucille and Sarah were inconsolable. Mrs Weston found she was more hurt than she thought she would have been and Frank and Peter also mourned.

It seemed the wrong time for Peter to announce that he would be marrying Lucille but under the circumstances no one thought it was timely to protest. Lester, who had come to offer his sympathy, took Peter aside and confided in him that he thought his father had been looking forward to training the boy so that he could help him in his business in the future, and now this was impossible. He explained to Peter all the plans his father had for expanding the business.

'Now he will probably not do anything and that would be a pity for the country as a whole.'

'Why do you think he won't?'

'Because there is no point in building an empire if there is no one to whom one can leave it. Unless you can commit yourself to helping him, he will probably shelve it all.'

'I have already told him I am prepared to help, and if he wants a greater commitment I am prepared to give it now. Since I am going to be married I will have to settle down and do what is best for everyone.'

'I am glad you see it that way, because I would like my children to return but I would not ask them to do so unless there were a bright future here for them. I know they feel the same way.'

'You are making me responsible for many futures but as I have already said I am prepared to help.'

★

'There is no need for sacrifice, Jan.'

'I know. Dan told me. You loved the boy, didn't you?'

'I am not sure. I am glad I asked Lucille to marry me before he died.'

'So am I. When did you ask her?'

'Yesterday.'

'Dan wants me to marry him. Lucille and Boy no longer need him. He intended taking them away.'

'There is still no need for sacrifice.'

'It isn't sacrifice. You and Lucille will be happy. You have found your solutions.'

'But you and Dan will be happy?'

'We are not made for that kind of happiness, Peter. I envy you. You need not worry about your friend. He thinks I intend to marry him and he will be happy for a while. It will be a glorious engagement. Then he will find the call of tomorrow too strong to resist. He has his causes, but if I can make him less bitter then perhaps his crusade will not be a hopeless one. He will have some memories to cherish and perhaps one day he will come back.'

'Isn't it a pity that love does not make both parties equally blind?'

'Hardly! Think of all the chaos that would result. In fact, all your tragedies appear to occur under those very circumstances. It is better to be only half blind. I have to thank you for my life and I don't know how to do this. I would offer to pay for the operation but I am certain that is not the answer. While my hair grows back I will try to think of something.'

'Don't bother! The satisfaction of doing good deeds should be its own reward.'

'That is not logical in a medical context. You would have me pay you only when you fail to cure me.'

'I agree it is illogical, but since I am not going to be a doctor for much longer I would like to cherish one valiant deed.'

'I will not deny you your triumph and I will try to get better quickly.'

Printed in the United States
125364LV00002B/313-330/P